GRYNNE, GRETCHEN

AND

THE CAPTAIN

THEIR FIRST ADVENTURE

GRYNNE, GRETCHEN

AND

THE CAPTAIN

THEIR FIRST ADVENTURE

BENJAMIN DOUGLAS

Published by Sixth Element Publishing
On behalf of Benjamin Douglas

Sixth Element Publishing
Arthur Robinson House
13-14 The Green
Billingham TS23 1EU
Great Britain
www.6epublishing.net

© Benjamin Douglas 2022

ISBN 978-1-914170-26-3

To Megan, Caleb, Rachel and Karis, with love

CONTENTS

Prologue... 1

1. Puzzles and Pirates 3

2. Marines and Memories.. 15

3. Looms and Dooms.. 38

4. Tapests and Times Lost.. 58

5. Messages and Memories 73

6. Birds and Battle-Play 87

7. Feelings and Forebodings 106

8. Blades and Trades 124

9. Hopes and Heart-Songs.. 145

10. Taverns and Tales 160

11. Marines and Menaces.. 173

12. Pirates and Preparations 191

13. Schemes and Dreams... 207

14. Battle-Barges and Charges 226

15. The Doomed and Marooned.................................... 243

16. Broadsides and Quaysides....................................... 261

17. Scrapes and Escapes.. 288

18. Good Tides and Brides.. 322

Glossary of Terra Words 329

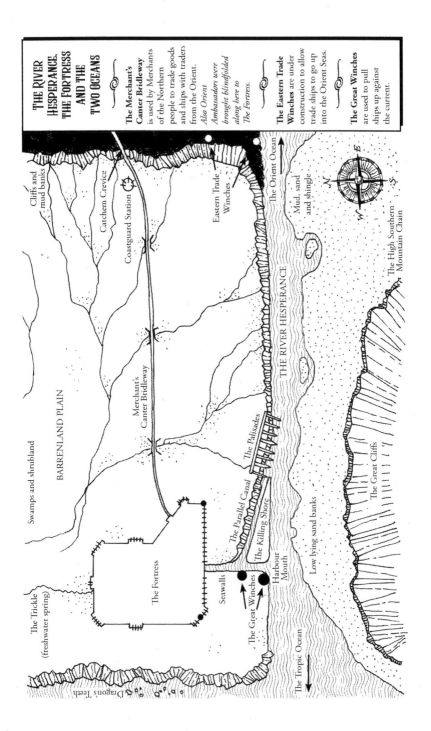

THE RIVER
HESPERANCE,
THE FORTRESS
AND THE
TWO OCEANS

The Merchant's Canter Bridleway is used by Merchants of the Northern people to trade goods and ships with traders from the Orient.
Also Orient Ambassadors were brought blindfolded along here to The Fortress.

The Eastern Trade Winches are under construction to allow trade ships to go up into the Orient Seas.

The Great Winches are used to pull ships up against the current.

Cliffs and mud banks

Catchem Crevice

Coastguard Station

Eastern Trade Winches

The Orient Ocean

Mud, sand and shingle

N
E
S
W

The High Southern Mountain Chain

BARRENLAND PLAIN

Swamps and shrubland

Merchant's Canter Bridleway

The Palisades

THE RIVER HESPERANCE

The Great Cliffs

The Trickle (freshwater spring)

Dragons Teeth

The Fortress

The Parallel Canal

The Killing Shore

Seawalls

The Great Winches

Harbour Mouth

Low lying sand banks

The Tropic Ocean

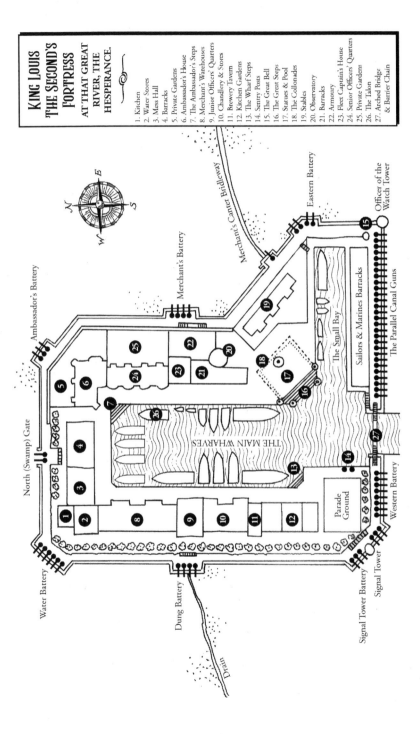

KING LOUIS THE SECOND'S FORTRESS

AT THAT GREAT RIVER, THE HESPERANCE.

1. Kitchen
2. Water Stores
3. Mess Hall
4. Barracks
5. Private Gardens
6. Ambassador's House
7. The Ambassador's Steps
8. Merchant's Warehouses
9. Junior Officers' Quarters
10. Chandlery & Stores
11. Brewery Tavern
12. Kitchen Gardens
13. The Wharf Steps
14. Sentry Posts
15. The Great Bell
16. The Great Steps
17. Statues & Pool
18. The Collonades
19. Stables
20. Observatory
21. Barracks
22. Armoury
23. Fleet Captain's House
24. Senior Officers' Quarters
25. Private Gardens
26. The Talon
27. Arched Bridge & Barrier Chain

Water Battery

North (Swamp) Gate

Ambassador's Battery

Merchant's Battery

Merchant's Canter Bridleway

Eastern Battery

Dung Battery

Drain

Signal Tower Battery

Signal Tower

Western Battery

Parade Ground

THE MAIN WHARVES

The Small Bay

Sailors & Marines Barracks

The Parallel Canal Guns

Officer of the Watch Tower

PROLOGUE

In the age of the 'Enlightenment', Copernicus, Galileo and a host of others had proven (or at least strongly-suggested) a number of revolutionary and disturbing things like the idea that the Earth wasn't flat, that it revolved around the sun, not the other way around, and they were just one 'group' of people propounding weird and wonderful theories. Amongst these were the concepts of alternative, parallel or other 'kinds' of Earth. Long-forgotten philosophers such as Boggle and Strewth, even claimed that it was not only possible to travel to and fro between these other worlds but that once Alchemists had finally discovered how to transmute lead into gold, they would therefore exercise control over the four elements and create life itself.

These visionaries suffered persecution and threats of death. Meanwhile on one such alternative Earth ('Terra' by name), in their year of 1798, our new-found friend Grynne, was quite puzzled.

1. PUZZLES AND PIRATES

Grynne lived on Drat Island and he'd often been told that he was a good friend. Gretchen had told him so and he knew that Gretchen was always right. He often wondered if he would ever see Gretchen again. In point of fact, he wondered about that mostly, but he had plenty of other things to do, to fill in his time on Drat Island, his home. Gretchen and Grynne often played puzzles of all different kinds. She would say something like, "He started a journey but regretted it before it was finished," and then Grynne would try to puzzle out the 'Who' 'What' 'Why' and so on, by asking questions to which Gretchen would only answer, "Yes," or "No!"

Gretchen could speak to animals she said and had many 'gifts' as she called them.

She talked in different languages and gave Grynne books and parchments to read and math problems to puzzle and solve. He had been so happy with Gretchen as he grew up on the island and when she said that she had to go away for a while, he did not know what to say. Two sea-vessels had recently washed up on False Bay Beach, a Qajaq from the far northern Eskimo peoples and a naval Skiff. Grynne had repaired the skiff and Gretchen had made new sails and ropes. It was their last project.

"Tomorrow," she said, "repair the Qajaq and learn how to paddle it, here's some tips."

Although it leaked quite badly, she had hopped in and

showed him some skills with the single paddle blade. When later, she came back to the beach, she was very wet!

When he woke the next morning, there was a note by his breakfast bowl. She was gone and he realised then that it would have been too hard for either of them to have said goodbye. He tucked the note into his folio of songs and wept a little. Two long seasons of winter gales had since passed, plus a short summer. He had grown taller and much stronger in that time. He missed Gretchen very much.

Nonetheless, he was content. He had the vegetable garden to tend, fishing and salting, egg-collecting, sea-bird-netting, berry-picking, jam-making, cooking, washing and the cleaning, plus keeping his old cabin well-maintained. It was very old and needed a lot of repairs to withstand the cold fury of the winter storms. The windows rattled in the wind and when they broke, it was hard to repair them with the sticky sap from the gum-tree, but he liked a challenge and they were now all different colours and shapes, which he liked. He loved his workshop even though it was very small, because in the good weather he repaired and made things outside on a ship's work-bench, under an old sail. He had lots of bits and bobs, boxes, bags and adventuresome things that might come in useful one day. Some he picked up from the beach after a storm, some he found in the bird's nests in the forests and high places. In the winter, he did weaving on his loom in the cabin, making cloth out of soft nettle-stem and Ivanchay weed or using tough sisal bracken to make sacks.

He made tunes and songs to the rhythm of the loom too. Some he thought were quite good. Gretchen had liked his songs and she often asked in the evenings if he would sing for her. Keeping his tools sharp and in good order and the little workshop dry in the winter, so that things wouldn't all go rusty, took a lot of his time. He liked spending time like that though. He once found big boxes on the beach full of swords and lanterns and guns. It took a long time to take all the salt and rust off them, but now they looked very nice on the wall. Large, leaky barrels, full of strange-smelling liquid often came onto the beach and he always put them in cold caves high up on the northern cliff-top, so that they would not poison the sea, or the land. The smell made him feel quite poorly as he carried them up, but he could not think of what else to do with them. Sometimes, old bones washed-up on the beach. He had found skulls and ribs, leg and arm-bones and so on. He knew they were from ship-wrecked seamen (or maybe even pirates), from far out to sea. He buried them carefully in a special, peaceful sunny place and planted flowers round-about. He often sat nearby and puzzled.

Walking up and down the mountain to the cabin, and ranging over the island, kept him healthy and he loved to see the flowers and the little birds and the beautiful butterflies all around him. He liked the sharpness of

5

the winter air, the white snows and the quietness that the snow brought and he also liked the warm summers' days. The trees were very interesting. Why were they all so different? And why did so few produce fruits and berries? Some grew only in high places and were bright colours; some only grew in low places and were mostly just green. Some grew together, some grew quite alone. That was interesting. That was a puzzle. He liked to watch the clouds and wondered at their different shapes. He noticed that their shapes changed according to the seasons and the winds, and he wondered why that was. Some of the clouds had faces or looked like fish; he often laughed at that as a good joke. Some of the faces looked fierce; he wondered if that was what pirates looked like. He had learned to predict the weather from clouds and their directions.

Grynne also liked to look at the stars and watch them at night. He would take a pile of soft grasses and small branches and make a bed out of doors on clear warm nights, lie on his back and count the stars. He noticed that some were bigger than others and different colours, or was it just his imagination? He counted up to 7,548 stars once but then fell asleep. Or maybe he just dreamed that he could count so high. Some of those stars were put so close, that they looked like things. Why would that be? he thought. The stars also changed their places during the year. That greatly puzzled him. But he liked being puzzled because he liked to think about puzzles. The big old sun really puzzled Grynne. He thought about the sun a lot, probably because he really liked the sun. In fact, he liked everything here. Drat Island was a nice place to be.

For most of the spring and summer of this year, Grynne had worked very hard and had also cut wood for his winter fire. Now it was the late autumn and he could take some time for himself and his songs. Gretchen had warned him about bad people and particularly, pirates. His cabin was high on the mountain and he had lots of rocks he could throw down if he needed to, but Gretchen had also told him that pirates would not be very likely to hurt a big guy like him. He could see the deep-water anchorages from his cabin, so he could see any pirates before they could land. He had never seen a pirate ship. In fact, he had never seen any ship close up. It was quiet where he lived. He was not afraid, but sometimes wondered if he should be. He could see a chain of rocks afar-off if waves pounded upon them and sometimes on a very clear day, he could see sailing ships beyond, but none ever came close to Drat Island.

One bright sunny day, with the wind fresh and strong at his back, Grynne was ambling along the sea-shore. He had ambled away from Dark Hill and climbed over Bouldery Bank. He was now halfway along False Bay Beach, the blue-green sand soft and warm under his bare feet. Today was a day to just amble.

Ambling along and over a dune, he looked down and surprised, he saw something new, something unusual. In fact, he saw several unusual things on the beach. One of them was a big ship, a square rigger with three tall masts, sails flapping. They cast very long shadows.

"Good heavens!" he said aloud. "I must have been ambling along for hours, it's late."

"Yes, it is late in the day and this long green beach…" said a very loud, deep and fearsome voice, "…is in quite the wrong place for a beach to be!"

Grynne jumped in surprise. He had not realised that one of the strange objects on the beach was in fact, a man! Now Grynne himself had a loud voice, and he was thinking what to do. Should he turn and run, or should he wait until the stranger spoke again?

"Well, what are you going to say?" The stranger was pointing at him.

Grynne was about to speak, when he realised that the stranger was not only pointing at him, he was also pointing a flintlock pistol at him!

"Yoicks! A Plintlock Ffistol!"

The stranger laughed and he slapped his thigh with his free hand and turned around, stamping his foot as he roared with laughter. Grynne was not a little cross to be laughed at.

"Well, you would say it so, if someone pointed a nasty thing like that at you, or, or, or threw a tree at you."

"Threw a tree?" spluttered the stranger. "Threw a tree?!"

"Yes!" said Grynne and in a quick temper, he tore up an old palm tree and in a fit of anger, threw it at the stranger!

"Aaargh!" The stranger fell backwards over an old, very battered sea-chest. The tree flew over his head, but some small branches caught him about the head, knocked off his cocked hat and left some leaves and part of an old birds' nest stuck in his long-faded ginger beard.

"Septacaemic Sea Serpents!" he shouted as he flailed about in the sand.

As the last of the palm leaves fell out of the sky, Grynne could now see two long black sea-boots and green pantaloons wiggling over the open lid of the old sea-chest.

He looked over at the stranger and not thinking any more of the flintlock pistol which was nowhere to be seen, he stepped around the old sea-chest, knelt down and held out his hand.

"Are you hurt? Can I help you up?"

The stranger with the ginger beard shook sand out of his hair, tossed aside the old birds' nest, wiped some more sand off his old cracked leather eye-patch and, spitting sand onto the beach, growled deeply... then laughed and laughed again until the air was full of sand and palm leaves and salty language. "Keel-haul-I for a landlubber!"

Grynne was now at somewhat of a loss, but the stranger's laughter was so free and happy that he quickly began to laugh as well. The stranger found his cocked hat and jammed it on his head once again.

Grynne held out his hand. "Well, I can at least give you my hand and set you back on your feet again," said Grynne.

"Sooner I'd be back on sea, if you please," the ginger-bearded stranger said, becoming more serious and speaking in that deep voice once again, but on his back and with his legs in the air, he didn't seem so fearsome now.

"If I do help you up, you won't shoot me, will you!"

"Shoot you? Shoot... ah now, my fine fellow, never you worry about that! Now my old pistol Brannigan... wheresit... whatever... old Brannigan! Slippery Anchors! Where's me pistol?"

Grynne found it by the sea-chest and unsetting the lock, warily handed it back.

"Well, I'm stood up now and no need of your kind offer," said the stranger, placing the pistol in its holster and adjusting his cocked hat.

"It was the least I could do. My name is Grynne by the way," he said, brushing sand off his fingers ready to shake hands, but before he could do so, the stranger beamed an old sea-dog smile and his one eye twinkled as he said, "It's a fine pleasure indeed to meet you, good master Grynne, and if I may now introduce myself: I am, sir, your servant, Captain Benjamin Witherspoon-Golightly of the good ship, Cleveland." So saying, he made a flourish and with one fine and lordly sweep, took off his hat and swept low to the ground in a courtly and majestic manner, his sword-tip brushing the sand. He paused momentarily for effect, stood back to attention, heels smartly together and then replaced his hat in fine style, back on his head, his long white hair (as if by magic) flowing elegantly over his shoulders.

Just like Gretchen's painting in my cabin up on Mortlocks Mountain… thought Grynne. Even the silver buttons of his jacket look the same. That's a puzzle!

"I, I really am quite sorry about the tree and the chest and, I fear your belongings have vanished into the sand. It is quite empty!"

Captain Benjamin Witherspoon-Golightly harrumphed softly. "That-there chest has been bereft of tackle and tin, for far too many tides, I fear."

"Pardon?" said Grynne.

"Hmm? Oh, to speak landlubber, it's been empty, for a long time. As I was remarked earlier, this is quite the wrong place to have such a beach." He gestured now to his ship, laying on its side in the shallows. "Quite the wrong place as I say. My sea chart shows open water here and a saving of some time for me but the old fool who drew it was fonder of his rum than he was of his sextant. Rest his soul!"

Grynne knew why this was known as 'False Bay', Gretchen had told him why, before she left. The blue-green sand looked like flat water if you were on the sea and approaching from the north.

The sun was by now very low in the sky and the shadows from the ship, the chest and the two men chased each other like black horses to the far end of the bay. A cool wind began to blow and the sails of the ship flapped and seemed to give Grynne inspiration as he suddenly shivered and said, "Now, Captain err, Banjamin err, Watherspume-Jo-jo…"

"Golightly!" said the Captain with a grin.

"Now Captain… I will atone for my temper by emptying your fine ship of water, sand and err, leaves and then pull it further up onto the shore. I'll also build you a fine fire. There seems to be an old palm tree just over there, quite suitable for that purpose!"

Well, the two men started to laugh again and they slapped their thighs just like old ship-mates at that joke and fairly fell about on the sand. Then Grynne proved as good as his word. The frigate Cleveland was soon emptied of its sand and water and dragged up above high-water-mark. The Captain was astonished. Grynne was amazingly strong.

The palm tree was also soon broken into pieces and the Captain took out his pouch containing flint, steel and dry tinder and by the time Grynne had gathered some sweet potatoes and scooped some small fish and crabs out of a rocky pool nearby, the fire was well-suited to cooking a fine meal. Some fallen palm leaves made a good covering to sit on the sand. Captain Benjamin Witherspoon-Golightly had said nothing while Grynne laboured, but he had kept a steady, single eye on him all the while. When their eyes had sometimes met, he grinned and rubbed his old faded ginger beard thoughtfully. There was something about Grynne, but he couldn't quite put his finger on it.

As Grynne gathered their supper, the Captain took out and cleaned his old pistol Brannigan.

When Grynne returned, he asked the Captain, "Do you have a knife?"

The Captain immediately handed him his old sea knife, silver and ivory hilt first and then settled himself comfortably back onto his old sea-chest, unbuttoning his leather and brocade jacket.

Grynne began to quietly hum a fine tune and before long he whistled a passage and without self-consciousness sang a few words of one of his nightly songs.

"Long, long shadows racing to the moon,
Late sweet winds blow softly down the dune..."

Stopping short, he asked, "Captain, do you mind if I sing?"

"Sing on, my dear fellow. You carry a fine tune."

"Sing stars of love, Sing, move my eyes afar..."

Such a song the old sea-dog had not heard for many a long year. The tune was similar to an old Gallic Oppra, he thought, and the words took his heart to a place almost forgotten. His eyes focused not on the horizon now, but on his old college, the shore-ship Excellence, hard by the Whitby Towns, high above the sheltered cove and protected from the Northerly gales by Guisborough Forest above. Happy times!

When Grynne finally let the last notes of his song fade into the breeze, the Captain found himself unable to speak. He applauded loudly instead.

"You'll stay with me tonight, in my cabin, will you, Captain?" Grynne said. "I see that you have a fine ship and all, but I'd really..."

"That I will..." replied the Captain, interrupting Grynne with a wave of his hand, "...that will be a delight and an honour!"

"It's a good cabin it is, good and dry and sound, with a comfortable guest-bed and all fine inside," Grynne continued. "Good and plenty of fresh clear air it has, though the southern breezes do tend to bang the door open, but they rarely blow here and never in the autumn."

The Captain nodded his head knowledgeably. "Aye lad, southern breezes are for spring voyages. 'Southern gales to catch the whales, when spring's a-calling, eastern blows bring icy flows, when winter's dawdling'." He sang more than spoke the old mariners' rhyme.

Grynne knew the tune and whistled it and they both laughed. As Grynne bent again to the task of preparing the fish for cooking on the glowing embers of the fire, Captain Benjamin Witherspoon-Golightly said quietly as Grynne looked up, "Good master Grynne, I could do with a friend like you."

2. MARINES AND MEMORIES

Captain Benjamin Witherspoon-Golightly slept and woke lightly. He always woke lightly. There was no sound. No sound except that of a deep and regular breathing. No one, not even a mouse, would have seen or felt him move very slowly and open his one eye. A finely engraved cutlass and a Spanail pistol were pointed at him! In a flash his own pistol was drawn and levelled at... at, at the... wall! The cutlass and a Spanail pistol were hanging there.

"Bother and Barnacles," he muttered and drew a proper breath, lowered his gun and took a better look around at his surroundings. He allowed himself a small yawn and stretched out on his bunk bed, as he did so. He had slept well and long. It had been a late but fascinating night.

The early morning sun filtered through the windows of the cabin. Crazy windows they were. Crazy is the only word that could describe them. Glass triangles and polygons of red and azure blue. Circles of amber and green. Parts of faces and landscapes, pictures built up of all kinds of glasses and resins and waxed or varnished papers, it seemed. Crazy and very beautiful. Beautiful was the word. Crazy, definitely! The morning sun was still low in the sky and cast its diffracted and modified light onto the wall by the side of his bed. He could now hear Grynne breathing softly in his sleep on the sofa-bed by the windows. Several swords and guns hung on that wall, while musical instruments and many other quite weird things hung on the other wall, the stone wall that had in it, a door and another window. What a window! Shaped like an Arabic arch, it glowed softly with reflected light from the orange-coloured soil that was Grynne's garden. It was more like a stained-glass window in a place of worship, than anything else. A riot of colours and shapes it was and, like the other windows, was made of many different and interesting things, broken glasses, bottles, barometers and other things of who knows what origin or manufacture.

Grynne stirred in his sleep and snored. Thereafter was the sound of deep and heavy breathing. His attention returned to the wall with the weapons hung so cleverly, so artistically.

"Whatever else you may be, good master Grynne…" the captain softly murmured, "…you have a 'good eye', as folk say." He rubbed his eye patch regretfully. On the wall by the door into the workshop, he now noticed a Sammury blade, that seemed to underline several cutlasses which hung vertically, some with point up, others point down. That Sammury looked familiar somehow, but no matter. It was old, very old indeed, but was still deadly, no doubt. Its scabbard had half of its embroidered covering torn away, and the blade was engraved with likenesses of slain warriors. It was more green than gold and matched the green lettering of the papers behind it. The Captain realised that the wall (all of it) was covered with packing-case papers of all shapes and sizes. He chuckled softly.

Grynne had removed the papers from washed-up boxes and used them as wallpaper.

"Ingenious," he said, so lightly that he would not disturb Grynne's slumber.

He walked softly over to the wall in his bare feet and studied the papers more closely. Advertisements of goods from the Orient, Indie and the far Northern Isles festooned that wall. Writings from every land, pictograms, cartoons, prints and stencilling met his eye. All of the words he could read. He knew every language and tongue and he smiled as he cocked his head on to one side to read the Japans' description of the pickled fish jars, that had at some time past, travelled in tough amalgam-wood boxes in the hold of a junk, on the low seas of the Orient. He liked pickled fish. I wonder if Grynne has any jars still left? he thought. A Georgian dagger caught his eye and his attention returned to the weapons. "What a fine and impressive collection of weapons," he breathed softly and stretched out his hand to feel the cold carbon steels, the dull gun-metals and inlaid golds and silvers, the carved woods and waxed leathers. He fingered the woven cords and lightly jangled the chains that held scabbard to belt and powder horns to straps. No short-swords here though. Not the collection of a real warrior. The collection of a beach-comber and a musician, he thought to himself but something gave him pause at that thought. He turned and regarded the sleeping form of his new friend Grynne. Not a warrior? Not yet leastways, he'd soon... he'd soon... Grynne shifted a little and the morning light lit up his face. Grynne reminded him of someone, someone… with a sudden start, he realised who and before he knew it, he was a young lieutenant again, many years and many sea-leagues away, in the doomed fortress guarding the distant Orient. Lieutenant Golightly, of his Majesty King Louis the Second's warship, Talon, stood at the small window of his quarters overlooking the banks of the great sea-river, the Hesperance. He served as ship's lieutenant and Chandlery-officer at the fortress of Louis the Second ('Louis the Unlucky' as he was now known, for his failures in both diplomacy and war). He saw again so clearly, the old battle-sea-chart on his wall (that he had re-drawn) with the new fortifications to what was only known as 'The Fortress'. It stood not one hundred and seventy-five yards back from the Hesperance. This linked the shallow Orient Sea to the Tropic Ocean of the northern peoples. His own people. The Tropic Ocean was two fathoms lower than the Orient Sea and so the river ran dangerously quickly down into it. Orient warships had long used this passage to gain access to the Tropic Ocean and to plunder the settlements and trading ships of the northern peoples, dragging their ships and plunder back up through a heavily-fortified chasm in the sea-cliffs to the North. The northern peoples had therefore allied together and had fought many bitter battles to capture the river bank to the north, in order to build the Fortress. Every Orient ship now trying to sail down the Hesperance was blown to pieces by huge cannons. They had soon learned their lesson. Two, heavily-damaged Orient warships had remained in the Tropic Ocean for some time.

Hunted by fleets of small cruisers, they skulked from place to place, with little food or ammunition left. Unable to surrender, due to their strict martial code, they eventually scuttled their own ships or blew-up the main magazine and went down with their ships gladly, so it was said. The Tropic Ocean and the trading routes of the northern peoples were now safe, so King Louis and his advisors thought. Negotiations continued with Orient Ambassadors who were led in and out blindfolded, to great feasts at the enclosed Ambassador's Residence inside the Fortress. Orient traders bartered their goods and ships for gold and silver outside the Fortress at the Coastguard Station near to 'Catchem Crevice' (named after Martin Catchem, the Craftsman-Engineer who built the Fortress to King Louis' own design). No Orient traders were ever admitted into the Fortress, so as to keep her defences and layout as secret as possible. Once a deal was struck, the traders sailed back on other vessels and their trade-ships were then lined down the Parallel Canal (as it was inaccurately called) into the Main Wharves and those ships never again returned to the Orient seas. All of this was good but nevertheless Lieutenant Benjamin Golightly, was in an ill humour.

I've been too long in this lousy fortified port for comfort, he thought to himself.

"Too long with comfort, ease and civvy-idleness!" he said out loud and his room-mate Harry Bessler stirred and woke with that.

"Bother and Barnacles, I've woken you again, Hal."

19

Ben always called him Hal, as was the wont of the northern peoples, to alter and shorten their given names, amongst friends.

Hal slowly rolled over onto his back, his long curly red hair, half-covering his handsome Celtic features. He rubbed his eyes, one green and the other an icy cold blue. Ben and Hal had been in this so-called impregnable fortress for six months now. The marines and seamen were fat, slobby and weakened by their excesses of cheap wine, watery-beer and oily food, and many now lay sick as a result.

"No gunnery practice for five months!"

His voice rose and this time Hal Bessler had awoken enough to respond. Ben leaned on the window ledge and looked out from their window. "It's not as if we've not plenty of powder and shot, but that fat, bloated fool of an Ambassador doesn't 'like loud bangs'... doesn't like loud bangs my eye. One of these days I'll..."

"So you say, and (yawn) say again! What are you (yawn) worried about? The war is over; no ship can gain entry or take a line against us and our (yawn) our good King Louis has given the order. 'Lay-by, stay safe in your haven, war is over and done. Should it ever come again, once more we'll prevail'. We're safe here, Ben, only one more month and we're back to Albion, to the shores of Old Blighty. We're SAFE, Ben..." he said scratching under his armpit. "...the old Hill fort covers the forests and swamps behind us to the north and the old Hesperance runs along so fast, that no ship from the north can gain entry to the harbour, except by the parallel canal and we control that with two hundred men and fifteen eight-inch cannon. Also (as you well know) that canal is blocked with the big palisades (which only we can draw up) and the canal is also festooned with rotating spikes that will sink any ship bearing down on them. Below all of that, are the ten-inch guns, and only our own ships can come and go on the ropes of the Great Winches. Sure our men are slow…" He yawned long and deeply and scratched somewhere else. "…slowww… slowww… slow and whew, that was a good long sleep. Slow and sloppy, but what of it? What of it again I ask? The garrison…."

Ben had not been listening, as he had been surprised by a strange sight to the east. He studied with increasing puzzlement, a strange, thick fog rolling slowly down the Hesperance. It had a green-ish tinge about it, he thought, and surely it was the wrong season for fogs? And why was it confined only to the river? Then the first ship came through it.

"Blow me down! Hal! Up and about you, haste lad, HASTE!"

Hal sat up in bed and looked over to the open window.

There Ben pointed. "A ship… two ships… a… a… battle-fleet Harry, a BATTLE FLEET is coming down the Hesperance!"

Hal rolled out of bed and stumbled over to join Ben at the window. Rubbing his eyes, he looked eastwards and saw them. Seven ships that were now coming out of the fog, their sails half-reefed, coming down the sea-river at a good twenty-five knots or more.

"Well, those crazy Orients are as daft as you are, Ben; the canal to the harbour is still blocked, see you, and held by the Garrison. Strange that the bell hasn't yet rung and the eastern battery hasn't fired either… But no steersman on this Globe can turn into our harbour at that speed. Even if they do fire as they pass us by, they'll see their own shot bounce back at them from the outer walls and if they fire high, they might cut down a few flying bald buzzards a mile behind us! Then they'll be pulverised by the ten inchers on the western ramparts. Ha!"

So saying, he laughed and barked with humour. "Come on, Ben, why the face? Although I do allow that it is rather strange. Maybe they've been drinking some of our watery-beer! HA!" He stretched, arched his back and flexed the lean, powerful muscles of his arms and legs. "Just watch the show as the new breech-loaders of the western battery sinks every man-jack of 'em!"

Ben though was stern-faced, brows knit with concentration. The approaching ships were steering a line as straight as a die. Half-reefed sails flapping loosely, set on the wrong side for the wind and not of themselves making any speed, only the Hesperance itself bore the ships along. Why on this tide and with the wind from the south-west, why? He reached for his telescope and focused on the lead ship.

"Why now, you bilge-rat? Why on this tide and the

22

wind from the south-west, why? Why... what on earth is THAT!?" He spied a tall spar, wrapped around with chains and with claws at the top. It was taller by half than the main-mast and was on the harbour-side of the ship. "Septacaemic Sea-Serpents, if that's what I think it is..."

Hal was not listening, but talking-over Ben's frantic rant. "What now, Ben?" Hal beamed. "Just enjoy the show, they'll be past us in a flash, wither shins-deep in the big waves and whirlpools and probably turn-turtle! We should see them swimming for their lives any... what's that? What is that on the lead ship?"

"That's clever, Hal! We're in for a fight if that's who I think it is, on the lead ship. It's an Orient flagship, Hal! Admiree Sogon's flagship if I've got eyes not gob-stoppers!" He now levelled his spy-glass at a stately figure a head taller than any of the others, with a long platted black beard and clad in green and gold silks with a Sammury sword tucked into a sash. The man held both of his hands high and studied the shore-line intently as his ship accelerated along.

Ben could now see the Admiral's sash, chains and battle-jewels across his chest. Sogon! "Blow me down, it is him."

Ben now flung on his weapons belt and was reaching for the ammunition-pack that hung on the wall next to his battle-sea-chart. Always close beside his bed, they were. Always close at hand. He threw his last ever words to his best friend, as he ran for the stairs. "The One be with you, ship-mate. Make haste and forget your dress

23

uniform, fight as you are, fight with our men, fight for our men and our King and for your life, my friend!" He was out of the door and pounding down the stairs before Hal spoke again.

"But, but this can't be, Ben." As Hal looked, Sogon dropped his left hand and the lead ship dropped its strange device onto what was known as 'the killing-shore', by the harbour entrance. To his horror and dismay, the claws on the big spar dug into the ground and slipped, raked up soil and rock and then held and held and the chains ran out, held fast and went tight. The ship, like a mighty war-horse suddenly reined-in, seemed to tense and shake! Shocked and unbelieving and even without a spy-glass, Hal could see that every man-jack on deck was lashed to mast, or rail, or hung as if for dear life, to their guns. Then that great and terrible ship, The Serpent, the flagship of the feared Admiree Sogon heeled over hard to starboard; its upper rails and decks flooded with water and it swung around, swung into the harbour mouth.

Sogon's right hand now fell and the huge spar was blown clear of the ship. The flapping half-reefed sails caught the south-west wind and full now, those sails propelled that awesome warship up and into the harbour. Orient seamen and Sammury warriors hacked themselves free from their ropes and ran to their battle stations. In seconds, the battleship was past the sentry posts, of the Great Winches. Already moving fast, the ship now cruised into the harbour, passing under the Arched-bridge, her sharpsteel battle-prow easily snapping the ceremonial barrier-chain from its mountings. Ladders, gangplanks and grapnels now appeared on the deck which literally swarmed with troops. Admiral Sogon cut the silken sash that bound him to the rear mast and moved but two steps, then planted his feet wide, as in battle-stance. His orders already given, he gave the merest nod to the commander. The commander shouted two words. Immediately the sails were loosed and flapped loudly as they spilled-wind, oars came from her sides and the steersman of the ship manoeuvred her into the wharves of the doomed Fortress town.

Marines on the shore ran as their officers shouted orders. Bells began to ring out and lookouts on the ramparts shouted and cursed. Volleys of shots from marksmen in the halyards of the great flagship raked the cobbled sides of the wharves. Men fell there and did not rise again. Not one hundred yards away, the guns of the Parallel Canal lay silent. Fixed to fire only down onto the canal, they were useless in this fight. Frustrated and horrified officers barked orders, contradictory orders. "Pull the guns out of their placements and run them to landward!" "Belay that, keep them where they are, or the Canal will be open to the rest of their fleet." "We can't fire into our own harbour, what about our own men?" "Send our troops to reinforce the harbour." "Nay, keep them here in case we're outflanked." Confusion and fear reined in chaos along from the ramparts. No one had anticipated such a strategy of attack, or of an enemy fleet entering the harbour wharves.

"BEN!" said Hal to the empty room as the Serpent let her first port-broadside rip onto the western shore. CARNAGE!

Fire-shot sent tethered ships instantly aflame, chain-shot ripped apart the old sailors and the powder-monkey lads scrambling up onto deck. Cannon balls did their deadly work just at the water-line. Ships heeled over, their lower decks flooding, guns now useless, pointing straight down into the water. Men slipping and falling overboard, cries, oaths and prayers all muted by the deadly thunder of eighteen guns firing at helpless targets. Rooted to the spot, unblinking, and unbelieving, Hal saw the next ship attempt the same manoeuvre as the Serpent. They however, lowered their Spar too late, snagged the western harbour wall and spun around. Helpless, they turned upstream and capsized. An entire warship, upside down in seconds and every man on deck, lashed in place! All were doomed, not one officer, sailor or Sammury escaped their huge sinking coffin. As it passed the western ten inch guns of the Fortress, the gunners opened fire, one gun missed, but three more sent cannon balls deep into the ship and it sank like a stone, amid great plumes of fire and smoke. That was the only time those guns were to fire for the northern peoples. Although they cheered, great horror gripped those gunners, yet still they stood to their posts as they watched the unfolding battle and listened to their squabbling, panicking officers.

The third warship, seconds later (lower in the water and shaped like a large beech leaf), managed the entry easily and then turned incredibly quickly into the small bay behind the eastern guns and alongside the Parallel Canal's Barracks. Oarsmen swiftly manoeuvred their ship eastwards to let rip their first starboard broadside. Opening fire now at point-blank range, into and through the rear un-reinforced timber walls, she fired round after round into helpless and terrified ranks of gunners and marines. Sammury then swarmed ashore and took their toll of the shocked and surprised defenders. Defenders firing from the Astronomical Observatory were cut down by archers, who moved quickly to secure the adjacent armoury. Horses at the stables, alarmed by the sound of cannon fire and the terrified screams of their young grooms, went into a state of panic. Several bolted and jumped the fencing surrounding their compound and ran headlong into the fray. Two were shot down almost instantly by the archers and the rest ran around wildly, trampling both defender and attacker alike.

The Serpent, meanwhile, continued her progress into the main wharves and now let her starboard cannon rip, as their marksmen in the halyards continued their deadly volleys onto the half-dressed marines and sailors on the shore. Two barracks went up in flames and another disintegrated as twelve cannon fired chain-shot and grape-shot onto thin timber walls. Harbour buildings such as these were cheaply built and were never designed to resist direct assault. Six cannon on her port side fed shot into the ships tied fast to the western quayside which quickly began to sink and burn.

As dust, debris and smoke blew into the window, Hal, finally free from his shocked stupor, turned now and lunged for his weapons and sea-boots which hung on the wall beside his bed. Realising that Ben was already on the quayside barking orders, he had barely grasped the shoulder strap of his ammunition belt, when a second port volley from the Serpent's remaining six cannon thundered-out. The entire bedroom collapsed down onto the lower floor, and walls and roof rolled over into the fortress chandlery. Fire engulfed him, as heavy beams and roof tiles crushed him beneath their overwhelming weight. He smelt tar, ropes, and sail-cloth, but could not even cry out his rage and fear, as light, life and hope left him.

Ben, meanwhile, was now running north along the quayside with a half-dressed platoon of men fumbling with their muskets as two cannon fired. He saw the chain-shot coming, so slowly, yet so fast.

"Down!" he yelled, but he knew that whatever he did, he could not save the men on either side of him. The chains wriggled, snapped, buckled and swung as they arced towards them. Blood and fire filled his eyes as he threw himself down as low as he could. Behind him, the timbers and thin brickwork exploded and rained debris all over him. Dust filled his lungs and he slowly rose, hacking and coughing, unable to believe that he still had legs and both arms. He groped forward, realising that he couldn't see through his left eye. It was painful and very wet, blood ran down his cheek and he held his hand to it, as a shot from the swivel gun on the warship bridge-deck lifted him off his feet. Pinned beneath fallen timbers and bricks, he kicked out and tore a hole in his pantaloons and his leg. Wriggling and heaving, he rolled free. Once more, covered in dust and debris, his throat dry and painful, he rolled again away from flames he could feel, but not yet see, and coughed, and spat his mouth and lungs free of dust. In spite of his revulsion, anger, pain and embarrassment, yes, furious embarrassment, for they had been caught like rabbits in their own burrow, he shouted aloud, "Damned-fine gunnery you…"

Another broadside from a third ship entering the Main Wharves drowned him out and a blast blew him head-over heels backwards into the debris and burning timbers. He rolled over and started once again very painfully to rise. Kneeling, he gathered his thoughts and began to plan how he could reach his own ship, the Talon, on the far side of the Wharves, cut her free of her moorings and with the east wind, swing her round. Surely HIS crew could fire back and give a good account of themselves. As he stumbled and ran over terrible sights and things he dared not give too much attention to, the smoke cleared and he saw the Talon swinging around in the wind on a single jib-sheet. Someone had thought of bringing their guns to bear on the Serpent, which was now slowly turning to port. Who was that on the Talon's command-deck? Ensign Sweetpeace it was, Sweetpeace to be sure, good man he was. There on the foredeck, standing tall, shouting orders, rallying their men and… dying…

"Oh no, NOOOO!" Time stood still. It was all silence now. How could it be all silence? Did he keep on running? Did he fall and rise? Golightly could never rightly say. All he could remember, was seeing his ship, his beautiful Talon disintegrate, as the point-blank starboard broadside of eighteen cannon all but lifted her out of the water. Men and their weapons spun high into the skies and fell into the water or onto shore. Fire burgeoned out of every deck-hatch and hole. Shattered timbers rose high into the sky and blasted the men close by on the quayside. Explosions began and continued as she turned slowly, slowly into the water as only a great ship can turn, ever so slowly, in her death-throes… helpless he was. Completely helpless.

"Noooo!" he said now. The years had barely dulled that awful pain. Deep sorrowful pain it was and shame. Yes, shame. He should have been there, he should have been able to do something more.

"What's that!" said Grynne, turning on the sofa-bed.

"Oh my word," said the Captain very softly. How very like Hal, Grynne was, he now realised. How similar of age and colouring and stature and accent. How he had turned over just like Hal had done. The Captain hung his head into his hands and unprepared for the force of these old memories, he could do naught but weep.

Grynne was all confused, but was up in an instant and held the Captain firm, as he reeled and would have slumped to the floor. Putting him gently in a chair, he made haste for some water and brought him a cup, placing it into the Captain's shaking hands. He held off from saying anything, but then made hot sweet tea and brought it to the red-eyed weeping Captain, who now stared at the window. In that window of all different colours and shapes, he saw faces, bodies, fire and smoke. He saw things that he had tried so hard to forget.

Later, by lunchtime of that day, the Captain had told Grynne of the massacre, how he and a few men had fought as well as they could, but had been driven back through the Swamp Gate and into the scrubland and swamps. There they lived as hungry, hunted men for many long days, scarcely taking a moment's sleep. They saw terrible things as their hated enemy burned-up shattered buildings and ships with corpses still inside and then burned-up the trees and bushes of the land, denying them cover where they might hide.

Grynne could see that the Captain remembered that time of struggle, with as much pride as sorrow, as he spoke of his comrades-in-arms and how they fought for each other. He explained that they knew that Orient soldiers would now be marching towards them from the northern sea-cliff bunkers of the chasm. The old hill-fort, originally built by Orient engineers, was lightly armed with only a handful of marines and relied on the cannon of the northern batteries of the Fortress for its own defence. Almost too quickly for belief, Orient gunners were pounding the old hill fort with the Fortress's own eight-inch cannon! Survivors quickly ran into the swamps and met up with Ben's men. They had almost no gunpowder or shot and no man was fully armed. They were caught in a classic 'pincer-movement'. They had no chance of survival if they stayed where they were. To both their east and west were treacherous sea-cliffs and no means of escape through the shark-infested seas of that coast. They could see the Coastguard Station burning and had no doubt that they were the only survivors of the Fortress. Orients took no prisoners.

Grynne was gripped by the tale and sat forward, attentive to every detail, with his hands clutching the arms of his chair. He nodded or shook his head as the tale unfolded, but scarcely muttered a word. He replenished the Captain's mug of tea as he drank it and once or twice he nearly swore, but he just managed to control himself.

One pitch-black night and in a fearsome easterly gale, the Captain and his men had dared to re-enter the Fortress and the harbour wharves. Sliding on their bellies, the stinking swamp-water channels were their only possible route. Swimming and diving where they had to, trying not to get caught in the roots and tendrils of the burned trees and bushes, they then 'laid hands' (as the Captain described it) on a whole patrol of Orient Sammury by the Swamp Gate. Taking their weapons, they then crept, dripping-wet, weak and sore into the semi-darkness, through the smoking ruins of the Ambassador's residence, then through the devastated barracks. Finally, after dealing silently with two more patrolling sentries, they reached the southern end of the chandlery buildings, which were now merely rubble and ashes. Amazingly, the Brewery Tavern was largely intact and many drunken Sammury lay asleep, in and around its smoke blackened walls, their traditional silken tents covering the kitchen gardens and the Parade Ground. There, by the Wharf Steps, they took a longboat from its sleeping crew and losing two men in a short fight, to the swords of a Sammury patrol, they pulled with ropes their craft under the Arched Bridge and beyond the entrance of the harbour.

Using every ounce of their remaining strength, as Orient archers killed two and injured three more of their number, they rowed out and ran the whirlpools and currents of that great river, the Hesperance, out to the open ocean and into many more trials and adventures that brought them eventually back to their own land Albion, seven months later. Seven men safely home. From the crews of nineteen ships and cutters! Out of two and a half thousand sailors, marines, engineers, politicians and merchants, only seven men returned home. Of them, only three ever sailed again and two more were eventually persuaded to join the Home Defence Forces, the 'Humdeefs' as they were known.

Grynne could scarce believe how any man could prevail against the trials of combat, yet more combat, then hurricanes and high water. But the Captain had prevailed and as he spoke even of his enemies, he did so with respect and little hatred. As Grynne listened, his admiration and love toward his new friend grew all the greater. The Captain now paused in his tale, as he watched a red triangle cast by one of the glasses in Grynne's window finally intersect a carved line in the stone floor. Angling his head curiously, he read what was carved alongside it.

"Midday...? MIDDAY!"

Then the clock struck twelve and the Captain stamped his foot. Grynne jumped and realised that he was by now, well-near frozen into his chair. His back ached as he moved and stretched.

"Well now! I've raddled and regaled you more than any gentleman should ever do and even my belly tells me that it is now mid-watch-meal-time. You fixed me a fine and rare meal last night, and a very fine meal at that it was." He rubbed his beard at that remembrance. "And now I must reciprocate!" He rose, pushed open the door to the corridor, walked into Grynne's larder and perused its impressive contents. It was very well stocked. "Aha! I'll take some of that and some of this..." Handling some vegetables. "...Yes... hmmm, that as well I think..." he said, reaching for an exotic fruit "...and mercy, you've some of those too." He put his selection of food stuffs and a large bottle of home-made juice into a woven basket and walked back into the cabin. Having plundered the contents of Grynne's store, he said not so much loudly as firmly but in a very kindly manner, "I'll now make you a very fine pickled fish stew, whilst you tell me more of your story and yes, tell me more of this pretty girl you know, this lassie that taught you all you know. What's-her-name, Gretchen (common name for a wench that is), Gretchen, was it now? You just open this fine bottle of juice and pour me a glass now, there's a good lad. Gretchen now. Tell me all about your Gretchen." He spoke softly and absent-mindedly hummed an old tune. He tapped an old earthenware crock that was full of chefs' knives, spoons and spatulas. Drawing out a selection, he laid them by the basket and reached for a large pot, hung by the stove.

Grynne, lost in his own thoughts, didn't hear the Captain's request.

"Good master Grynne! Gretchen now. Tell me all about your Gretchen." The Captain paused, turned and drew from a buttoned inner pocket, a small pewter and glass tube, his personal 'spice-vial'. Holding it up to the light, he tapped it twice or more and then screwing it open with some difficulty, he sniffed its contents. A great smile lit up his face and his eye gleamed. "Best spice in the northern hemisphere!" he shouted. "Best spice it is too, me lad-o for pickled fish stew!" he said again, grinning over at Grynne, who startled out of his reverie, laughed and slapped his thigh. "Come now, lad, and tell me all about your Gretchen." The Captain dropped the vial into the basket and tested the edge of a knife against his thumb. Satisfied, he began to pare and to chop some shallots.

"Aye aye, Captain…" beamed Grynne. "Gretchen Le-

Fay is her proper name and now I'll tell you all about her." As Grynne spoke, the Captain's eye caught sight of a small painting in oils and silver thread that he'd not noticed before, a painting of himself, Captain Benjamin Witherspoon-Golightly in profile.

"Le-Fay?" The Captain started. "Gretchen, LE-FAY!" he shouted, knocking the basket onto the floor as a southerly gale banged the door open!

Far away, her busy hands stopped. Far away and far below the ice, in the smoky whale-oil lantern light, her eyes focused not on her work now, but instead upon her past and upon the future, the coming battle. She saw again in her mind's eye, a small pewter and glass tube. A 'vial' he had called it. A spice vial he had called it. Precious it was to him, as was she. She knew that well.

Deep down now was she, hidden and surrounded by the cold arctic wastes and sea-glaciers of the southern archipelagos. Deep down and guarded by the lava flows of Atoll Dubh, which sent plumes of white smoke and steam into the air. Hemmed-in was she by the sharp, black and green obsidian cliffs, bluffs and the inaccessible pinnacles of 'The Impregnable Land', as the Sammury and Guards called it. Below in the dry-caverns, the forges and machines of the weapons cavern clanged an irregular muted-rhythm. In the loom cavern, the weaving looms hummed and banged out their own more musical rhythm. Wool and linen shanks of every hue, gold, silver and fine metal wires swayed in time and glinted on the walls and in the baskets. Shuttles knocked and rang as over forty Weaving-girls 'mouthed' their conversations over the row. Adept at lip-reading one and all, the girls could 'talk' over any noise and could 'hear' over any distance that they could see.

"Gretchen Le-Fay!" His voice rang clearly to her over the miles, as clear to her as if she had been in that same old cabin. She knew his voice, knew it of old, knew it so very well. She flinched and barely managed not to cry out in joy. Benjamin was with Grynne! Her sudden intake of breath was not seen by the nearby Blue Guard who shambled past her, half-asleep, not an arm's length away.

"So," Gretchen said softly. "So, Captain Benjamin Witherspoon-Golightly, we shall meet again and we that labour here will be ready. May the One speed you here, my LOVE."

And the girls saw her lips move.

3. Looms and Dooms

"You didn't tell us that!

You sly little vixen! It must be time then, is it time for us?

Sometimes me always did suspect of sometink of her like…

Well fancy, LOVE… and her being so po-faced and primly-pickled!

Oer, I'm not sure if I'm ready for this!

And can't she have a little spice in her life now?

Spice? I think it's more like a SPOUSE she's after… haaa!

Listen to you now, can't keep your eyes off that little guard with the squint-eye…

Hold your tongue, you raggedy-brimmed auld Biddy! I'll scuttle your Knot for you!

Time for us to dance upon the necks of those Blue Guards, is it now?

Called him-shanks 'My love' Wis that it, wiz her said?

Sometinks me hopes for mazelf, but I'ze plus olden now.

Well, I'm pleased for her, worked hard for us she has…

I'm up for a fight now myself to say!

Watchit girls, they've spotted us! Batten that squabble down…"

Hush!! mouthed Gretchen. Before she could even blush, the 'news' was all around the looms. 'My LOVE' was out of her mouth before she could stop herself. That was awfully unguarded. She was annoyed with herself, not to say… quite embarrassed! Worse still, the Blue Guards had spotted something. Now they would come down hard on any 'talking' that spoiled the rhythm of the looms and the rhythm had changed, the work had slowed. Two girls were hit on their heads by the guards over to her left, Paula and a girl also called Gretchen. Another Loom-girl, Tegan, was nearly knocked out of her chair by a blow to her side. All around she could see Blue Guards moving, some bleary-eyed from their slumbering, not a few being clubbed by their own overseers (now THAT was something good to see!). This was bad however, and getting worse by the second and it was all her fault! At the end of the second row, she could see the sadistic Brumuelr raising his staff to hit Sheelagh-No-Tears, the girl who refused to cry no matter what anyone did to her. All work on the looms had ceased now, the 'silence' was split by cries, curses and the sounds of beatings. These were her girls and she had to do something fast.

"Stop! STOP this NOW!" Gretchen's little voice somehow filled the whole stinking, humid cavern. Thinking faster now, she contemplated a terrible beating for herself but how could she stay the beatings of the others girls and prevent a dreadful discovery? She stood now, mouth open, mind racing… what to do? Overseer Brack Three stormed out of his Cot-alcove and the Blue Guard nearest to him flinched as he leaped aside, desperate to get out of his way.

"This, this work is due, err, overdue to Brigand Olliot," she said, pointing to her own and the other looms. "Beatings will only cause more delay, Overseer Brack Three. Return your men to their posts and we will continue with vigour. Do not delay us, I say. Are you keen to remain as Overseer or not?" She had gone too far, far too far, deliberately too far!

Overseer Black Guard Brack Three strode towards her, unsheathing his whip from his harness.

At least he'll bash me and not them, she thought. Stupid old… Then inspiration struck.

"It's all my fault, Overseer Brack, it's all my fault. I… I passed wind and said a naughty word, the girls heard me and…" Lavatory humour was the only humour that the guards had. Several of them guffawed and nudged each other in the ribs. They scoffed at her language and mimicked. "Passed wind!", "Naughty word," as their thick, stupid laughter uproariously filled the cavern.

Brack Three's stride faltered. He reached her as he began to laugh himself. "You little maggot," he spat out, shaking his head, hands now on his hips, faking an aristocratic woman's walk. "Proper little madam-maggot."

His men, impressed by his outstanding use of language and acting prowess, fell about laughing.

Faking fear, with far more skill than Brack had in his entire body, Gretchen shrank down onto her knees in what appeared to be abject terror. "Please, Overseer Brack, forgive me, I…"

Brack, moving as quickly as he could, swung his whip

against her head. Gretchen, not moving at a quarter of the speed she could move, took the blow and moved her whole body to absorb most of the impact.

She spun in mid-air and struck the floor, left hand hitting the floor hard to make the maximum noise, whilst her other hand sent a creel-basket spinning into the air. Falling back against her loom with her head, her foot banged the floor as hard as she could and the CRACK echoed around the cavern. She lay very still, bleeding from the side of her mouth. As a display of acrobatic legerdemain, it was as fine as any of the girls had ever seen. Several nodded approvingly and smiled behind their hands.

"Od's Blood! I've killed her!!" Brack muttered, slack-jawed and slobbering, the colour draining out of his cheeks. His skin, no longer dark blue, had faded to a pale grey.

Almost death-grey, thought Shelagh-no-tears as she suppressed a smirk.

Brumuelr, his deputy, had by now reached Brack Three (and was gloating, because he wanted to be the Overseer). "If 'n she be deed now Bra...err Overseer Brack, Brigand 'ul 'ave your 'ed on a spike! She be as best of the Loomers like and she teaches all the other trades like as best as too!"

Brack knew that all too well. His predecessors Brack One and Two stared down at him, dead, grinning and crumbling, spiked to the cavern roof, over by the blue door. He never looked over that way. At a loss now to know what to do, or to think (his normal state, to be frank), the looms now silent, his guards terror-struck as their lives were also now at stake, he jumped when one of them dropped a club onto the floor. What to do?

Shelagh-no-tears now pushed aside and ran past a huge guard, and kneeling down, pulled Gretchen to her breast. Other Loom-girls catching on to the charade, also flew to her side and in a gaggle of shrieks and tears with loud fretful voices, made a bad situation into a caterwauling and frenzied DISASTER! It was remarkable how everybody played their part so well. Gretchen opened one eye and, grinning at Sheelagh, said, "I'm okay. That big lummox barely grazed me."

"I know that well enough, you old ham. Knocking that creel into the air was a nice touch though, I have to admit. Keep it going a bit longer, girls…" she said, just loud enough not to be heard by Brack and Brumuelr. "Pandemonium is good for the soul, haaa!"

Several of the girls had to stifle a laugh and two giggled, just a bit.

"Okay girls, time to rise and show this blood all over my face," said Gretchen as she was raised with very wobbly legs back to her feet.

Her fresh blood now wiped deliberately over her cheeks and forehead, plus the scars and burns that spoiled her face, she looked quite spectacular now.

Brack, still pale but now visibly relieved and summoning his strength, re-asserted his tenuous authority as he cleared his throat. "Aar… harumph, now then back BACK

TO WORK, LAZY LOOL LATS, err I mean LAZY TOOM LATS, COOM LATS…" Deep intake of breath, "…LOOM RATS!!!" The last "LOOM RATS!!!" was truly thunderous and awe-inspiring.

Most of the girls were by now on their way back to their looms and several jumped at his bellow. Any humour was instantly dispelled. Cavern guards and their overseers were the lowest of the Orders apart from the Brown Guards who were fit only for menial work but they could all certainly shout. Whilst the Sammury were all Orient men and women, the Guards were… well… certainly not human or Terran. They were 'made' in the lower caverns in great secrecy. All of the girls apart from Sheelagh-No-Tears had been terrified of the Guards before Gretchen had arrived and taken control over the several trades and their respective caverns. Gretchen had turned mindless and fearful slavery into cool awareness. Awareness of what was really going on and how they could prepare themselves not just for liberation but to end the cruel tyranny that had brought them all here and threatened so many others.

Progress had been slow, agonisingly so, but progress had nevertheless been made. Good progress. The girls were still tearful and unsure at times but the evidence of Gretchen's wisdom, knowledge and downright low-cunning was all about them. Since she'd demanded to meet the Isle-Master Brigand Olliot and returned alive (the only Loom-girl to do so) there had been improvements in food, the all-essential ice-allocation and rest-times had actually increased. Above all else though, was the Dance! The Dance. Who could have imagined that Gretchen could introduce the dance, or how she had used it to transform the girls' lives. Brigand Olliot had been convinced by Gretchen that the Dance alone could keep at bay the dreaded scurvy that had previously afflicted the girls and diminished the output of the looms and other trades. That was partly true but it was really the addition of the bog-spices, fungals and seaweeds from the shore above, that Gretchen had added to their diet, that had in reality, banished scurvy from the caverns.

Time had rolled-on by since that time and though their imprisonment and forced-labour was hard to bear, there was now a good spirit in them all. Many of the girls had come from cultures and clans where the dance was at least a small part of their lives. Many had been trained to dance singly, or in groups and troupes as a preparation for adulthood, marriage, and the miscellaneous traditions of their peoples. Petite and very feminine though many were, because of the introduction of Gretchen's dance training, they were all now 'Judoka'. Few had heard of or trained in unarmed combat style previously and many had felt themselves incapable of achieving any prowess. Now however, after so many months of effort (and to admit it… a lot of FUN) they were ready. Waiting. Itching-to-go. Ready! Those guards were in for a quite a shock. As the girls began to pick up again the threads of their weaving, studying again the intricate patterns, complex pictograms, pictures and shapes on their pattern-skins, each was careful not to look at another. Heads bent low, hands busy with thread and wire, some taking pots of luminescence to finish some areas, they waited and waited until the guards fell to their customary manner of lounging, wandering and slothful chatter.

Overseer Brack Three's hacking cough echoed from his solitary Cot-alcove by the ice-stores, regularly punctuating the rattling drone of the machines. Slowly, slowly, 'normality' returned. A sly glance at the guards revealed that several were already asleep. Some crunched a handful of ice from their ration-boxes, resuming their dull, repetitive 'conversation'. They spoke of ice, food, sleep, fighting, beatings and not much else. Made in the breeding caverns, and selected for Brown, Blue or Black Guard training and duties according to their level of intelligence, which varied enormously. Some were in fact, re-cycled! None of these cavern-guards would ever see the daylight that the girls had been snatched from.

Gretchen now worked afresh and quickly, with her hands and her mind. Her own Loom-work occupied but a third of her time, yet she made the same number of Tapests per rotation, as the other girls. Otherwise, she drew patterns, corrected work, checked the dixies of dyes, paints and fasts and tended the long narrow trenches that produced the fungals that made such a difference to their collective diet. Beyond and above that, she recorded, reviewed and assessed all of the information that she collected on her trips between the caverns.

She looked now at her coded Tapest skins of plans,

maps, troop numbers and deployments and reflected that her own tactical plans were incomplete now only in small detail and merely awaited the arrival of the Cleveland, its crew and… a small and indistinct but unique light at her feet distracted her. A Ghecko stood there and blinked its eyes again, reflecting the light from the large candle at the end of her loom. She dropped a hank of wool on the floor and whispered to the little creature, "Meet me in the corridor, mind how you go!"

The Ghecko now moved slowly in the shadows towards the door, changing its colour as it passed boxes, creels, wools and other materials. Picking up the hank and looking to her left, she clicked her tongue and Sheelagh looked her way. Checking that none of the guards were looking their way, she mouthed through the din,

"Ten loom wefts and we'll meet.

Thanks, Maghoul, sorry I let slip.

Are you hurt?

That's okay, Maghoul, but did you actually hear your name, your real name?

Yes!

Wow!

Ow zoon ee comme sometink zoon? asked Megan who had spotted the 'conversation'.

I don't know but we must be ready,

I thought we were ready! said Old Sall.

There's more to do yet!

Right… couldn't be that easy now, could it? Several of the Loom-girls laughed silently.

Keep calm, my dear ones, but spread the word, Maghoul, we dance tonight.

Leave it to me…"

The only clue to what transpired over the next few minutes was a small but definite rise in the speed of their weaving. Smiling or frowning, every girl knew and knew that there was more to do, that they could and they would do more, prepare and anticipate it. Freedom! The dance tonight would be special, hard and most likely dangerous but the dance was the thing. Being Judoka was the thing! Times were a-coming, they were a-coming and… Please the One… soon, could they soon see their own families in their own lands again… please!

Her eyes strayed over to Overseer Brack Three and Brumuelr who were in conversation by the door. Squinting through the smoky light, she read their lips above the din of the looms.

"All kinds of darned new things, bothersome orders, changes to our ways… old Brigand Olliot like as 'im down as a trouble-maker like… don't care for his manner either, mind you… we'll 'ave to get these lazy guards up tae fettle quick-like… what's that northerner's name? Lord Nesbitt, as I've 'eard tell like."

Gretchen flinched involuntarily. It was a shock but somehow, not a surprise. It had been a long, long time since she had either heard or spoken his name and this time she kept her mouth shut! Nesbitt! she thought, that greedy, cowardly, toe-rag of a traitor who had betrayed the Fortress into Sogon's hands all those years ago. One of only two survivors of the attack and the only one not to face trial by combat with Sogon's Sammury, so she had heard. There had been whispers amongst her contacts, that he had either been accorded the honour of ceremonial execution and entombment with the Emperor's family or had risen to some high rank within the Orient leadership. So, high rank it was and he was here! Control… self-control, she thought, do not react. She remembered that as well as the usual traffic of transports and whale-boats, that there had been a smaller, faster cutter in the dock a few days ago… trust him to travel in style!

Removing now her own completed Tapest from the loom and touching for the last time the gold and silver threaded calligraphy, she checked the Birch resin that held a precious sapphire firmly into the woven headscarf-earpiece of the noblewoman that her work now honoured. Gretchen placed the Tapests carefully and with great pride into an oak cambrel. Her work mattered very much to her, all of her work. Even though this and many another of her Tapests honoured the ugly, dim-witted women of Brigand Olliot's people and bolstered his evil, cowardly reign, what she did, she did well. Very well. Picking up a handful of ice and faking a new limp, she headed for the door with the cambrel under her arm. There was no telling if any of the guards now remembered Brack's whip hitting her face, or her spectacular fall.

Best be careful and act as if at least slightly hurt, she thought to herself. As she went, she checked the girls' work on her aisle. She kept the youngest and least experienced girls closest to her. A word here, an adjustment to a loom there, checking the yarns at every station. "Show, teach and always encourage". Her mother's voice echoed to her down the years. This encouragement was no act to Gretchen and was completely natural. Well, when you were 437 years old, you'd learned a thing or two.

The Blue Guard on duty at the door (as ever gawping childishly), opened with some effort the huge iron-bound and graven door to the passageway. The door groaned and screeched on its hinges. Outside she showed her right-of-passage talisman to the Black Guard on duty who (woken from his slumber) grinned at her. The passage was narrow, long and curved to the left. As she went along, she secretly crushed small amounts of ice onto the floor so that if the guard should follow, she would hear the ice being crushed under his wooden clog-boots. Her own soft felt slippers made no sound and she walked quickly to a place where the efflorescence that lit the passage was dimmest. The Ghecko was waiting, almost invisible in the shadow of a riven slate. At her word, the Ghecko shivered and shed a portion of skin from its tail. Gretchen picked up the featherlight skin and quickly folding it, hid it in her bodice. The Ghecko rubbed against her hand and then scampered away. She smiled at the little creature and wished it well. "Thanks, little one, you don't know how important this is!"

Walking onward into the dimness, Gretchen could see small quartzite veins in the rock of dolerite, a very hard rock that had been quarried wherever found and used in the inner and outer defences. There were also tourmalines, a few gemstones and rare metals that intruded through faults and splits in the rock strata.

Steam also came gushing out of vents in the floor as she walked-on and in places she could hear the pounding of the waves above on the dark riven beach upon which she had landed all those long months ago. In some places, because of the steam, she could hardly see six feet in front of her but mostly, it was just a little dim. Passing the black stone outcrop, she counted seventy double-strides and stopped. Silent now for a few seconds. No sound from before or behind. Peering around the bend, there was a discarded block of dolerite. Twenty yards along from there, a soft, squelchy boggy area where her precious mushrooms and lichens grew, those precious things that had improved both the diet and spirits of her girls. Only she could spring across dry-footed. She looked about. No one stood there.

A quiet sigh and she knelt. Gracefully sweeping her long skirts above her knees, she bowed her head to the floor. Eight hours. Eight long hours at the looms. One more rotation over. Another Tapest and very important Tapest it was too, had been made. Her girls were still protected and safe through their unique labours... so far. She stared at the Cambrel at her side and visualised its contents. Three Tapests, to all intents and purposes painting/tapestries with a beautiful lady centre-stage, surrounded by images of her 'place' in the aristocratic world. Inlaid with precious metals and gemstones, they were luminous, three-dimensional and practically indestructible. The most important one was for the Lady Crimson De Dybrovnik. Some of her own hair had been ritually cut and woven inside her Tapest along with blood and… well, along with things that only Gretchen and three of the other Loom-girls knew anything of. The Tapests held or led to… another place where time didn't exist and precious things could be hidden.

Now for herself… One moment. One moment with the One alone. Later… perhaps an hour, maybe a minute, just one ring on a standard candle, she rose. Refreshed now, purposeful and focused. Dust shaken from skirts designed to hold no dust, she rounded the corner. Refreshed and elated now, she ran and sprang easily over the boggy-patch and landed at a trot. She held the Cambrel close to her and slowed to a walk as she approached the Black Guard. These were a different 'colour' in every sense of the word to the Blue Guards. Exactly ten double-paces from him, she moved over to her left and grinning with anticipation, stood in front of a large slab of dolerite. She began to slide her feet slightly over the sandy ground to make the sounds that a normal woman would make when walking. The Black Guard stiffened almost imperceptibly and then whirling so fast that a Blue Guard would have thought that there were two of him, he brought one of his three weapons to bear at her.

Which one will it be today? she thought. Lance, sword, dagger-throwel, or even his shield? The throwel was aimed at her midriff.

Rat! thought Gretchen. That would make for a slow and painful death… Just like a sadistic Troll! Just what I hoped he'd do.

The throwel was on its second spin, as she moved with practised clumsiness to the side as it slashed a ribbon free from her waistcoat.

"Why do you do that!" she screamed to hide the sound of the throwel hitting the rock behind her.

"Why do you'se insist on sneaking up on I, loom-maiden?" he said leering at her.

Black Guards were the closest to men in their desires…

This one fancies himself… fancies that I fancy him… Dolt! she thought and shouted, "I don't creep, I walk! and if that, that thing had have hit this Tapest, your nose would have been nailed to the Death-wall by Brigand Olliot himself!"

"Don't you take his name on them pretty little lips, gutter-wench. Loom-mistress and craft-maiden you may be… and a pretty little trim-rigged doxy-o to be sure… and I'se have my nose nailed, if I'se coulden nail you!" He slapped his thigh, then laughed and bellowed at his own joke… just like a Black Guard. "You'se faster than any Orient bilge-rat that I'se seen and I'se never gotten anywhere near you'se with any weapon, now has I?" Again, he laughed and bellowed as his sides trembled with stupid mirth. His oily, fishy breath made her nose twitch.

There it is again, thought Gretchen. They're all constructed from whale meat, gristle and boar-grease in vats of unspeakable filth by the foul magic of the

Maesterii Overseers and then somehow… endowed with some kind of spirit and a life of sorts.

A year ago, she'd slipped into the breeding caverns, after a Cider-Celebration on completion of another batch of a thousand Guards. All the Brown Guard-workers and Maesterii were asleep. What she had seen in the caverns then still made her tremble! His laughter now made her ears ache but the mental picture that she had just imagined of him and his ilk made her gag… just for a split-second. Then…

"Laugh all you like, Black Guard-Robert-Two, mark you well my talisman." She waggled it before his dull grey eyes. "You will let me pass with neither delay nor molestation if you please… oh and by the way… if I'm not mistaken, your throwel-thingy lies shattered on that dolerite-vein behind me!" She'd been saving that stratagem for a day like today (her Benjamin was on his way!) and today was that day! Letting the talisman drop back into her bodice and with a graceful stride, she went right on by him.

Not a jostle, not a grope, not a pinch, not even a leer, he stared glassy-eyed and appalled at the shattered blades and heft of his Guard-Clans oldest heirloom-weapon.

"Ohh… nay… nay. Od's blood pleeassse… I'se doomed!"

Guard-Robert-One (his predecessor, most of what was left of him) was nailed to the wall by the door. No one could quite remember why he had been 'disciplined' two years ago but there he hung as proof, if proof be needed. He did appear now, to grin!

"I can have that re-fettled and tempered for you, if I find you're of a courteous mind… if you're kind to me… and have a platoon-flagon of best cider for me when I return," she called over her shoulder to him, as she skipped into her long stride towards the upper cavern. She heard him wailing and cursing behind her.

"…an 'ole platoon-flagon of zider! Od's blood!!"

She shimmied and waltzed along with the Cambrel clutched to her chest as she turned the bend. "…if you're nice to me…" she sang to herself and giggled. He would have to grovel and lie, grovel and trade precious favours with his Guard Sergeant for a platoon-flagon of his best cider. That would make the Loom-girls', her dear Loom-girls' meals more tasty and add precious nutrients to their diet. Sweet… sweet was that thought! Her eyes shone like diamonds, in the half-light of the smoky lanterns (that burned better oils than she had to cook with!) that lined the lower corridors to the various caverns. She moved onto and up the old rock-hewn stairs, to the upper wooden stairs made with timbers taken from the ancient warships that had conquered these icy lands. Panelling made from those ancient keels lined the walls here and through the old ships' latticed windows, she could hear and see reflected patterns on the ceiling from the waves of the cold southern-ocean, crashing against the black rocky shoreline. A narrow breakwater and dolerite retaining-wall held back the sea which pounded onto the shore, moving the seaweed kelps like the motion of a woman's hair in a breeze.

Looking about and daring discovery, she left the Cambrel concealed behind a rock and pushed through the old fabric-curtains and sail-cloth drapes that held back some of the cold winds. Leaping over the retaining wall, she stood by the sea. Salt-spray and seaweed! They smelled so good and fine after the latent stink of the lower caverns. She filled her lungs with those airs, cleansing them, tingling with life and real light. How long now before her beloved girls could join her here and re-take their freedom? How long? She breathed deeply and stood facing the sea, the wonderful cold, spicy sea of the southern-ocean. The noise of the breaking waves was huge in her ears. Rainwater-ice in the freezing-pools above her creaked and shattered in the wind. Steam and hot water plumes boiled from the lava-vents near the shore, feeding the only place where seaweeds could grow and flourish. Now she laughed and sang, sang out loud an old tune almost forgotten now, remembering long wonderful nights in the singing taverns of the Old Whitby Towns.

"Were ye, were ye frae the brae? Were ye frae the brae?
Were ye frae oor olden brae? Gan ye to oor olden brae?
Birk and hull. Sail and storm-winds, sail on to warm winds

Where ye, were ye frae the brae? Were ye frae the brae?
Were ye frae oor Fernie brae? Gan ye to oor Fernie brae?
Birk and hull. Sail and storm-winds, sail on to warm winds."

Stopping then… before her voice failed and broke with raw emotion, emotion that was simultaneously old and new and so deeply felt, she heard as if by magic, her own voice rebound from the sea and echo between the shattered and salt-worn rock walls behind her…

"Birk and hull, sail and…"

Far away to the north in Grynne's cabin, the Captain had found a sheaf of songs and fancies written in Grynne's own hand. Some were well known to him but the Captain could see that most were of Grynne's own invention. One drew his attention and he noticed that its chorus was from an older song and he said, "Play this one for me, lad, if you please."

Smiling broadly, Grynne took the scrap of paper from the Captain's hand (an old can-wrapper of Bombay peas it had once been) and looked at the title. He turned and taking his 24-string Dulcimore from the wall and sitting down, he laid it on his lap and checked that it was in tune.

Hmm… a stickler for accuracy, thought the Captain.

Grynne played first the tune. It was fine and pleasant to the Captain's ear and reminded him, somehow… of the sea, its rhythm and pulse, its very… soul. Then Grynne took breath and sang…

> *"I'll be near, though far away,*
> *I'll be true as night and day,*
> *Wait on me and tarry nay,*
> *Time will show, we'll face the fray,*

"Benjamin, my love…" she half-thought, half-prayed and all-but shouted, "…can you …hear me now? Oh! can you hear me now?" The last words were more sobbed, than spoken.

Far, far away to the north, Captain Benjamin Witherspoon-Golightly did hear. Heard something so soft and musical outside… or maybe, was it inside? Grynne also heard and turned his head so quickly that his elbow knocked the ladle in the pot by the fire and tipped some fish stew onto the floor. He stood immediately and, holding the Dulcimore, he walked to the open door.

"Blow me down…" He was picking up the Captain's turn of phrase. "I could have sworn I heard her… but there's no boat, no ship. She couldn't…"

"That there was her, my lad. She knows!" the Captain said with warmth and much satisfaction.

"Knows what?" said Grynne, neither for the first or last time, well puzzled!

"Knows that we know and that we're coming to her… to the Factory Fortress… to Atoll Dubh!"

4. Tapests and Times Lost

The Lady Crimson de Dybrovnik flowed into her outer chamber. Behind her, serving-girls and lackeys flew to their tasks. Strewn clothing, rejected and torn scarves, jewellery tossed on the floor deemed to be "Too... too pale for my complexion... you OAFS!" littered the rugs and furniture of her apartment.

With a cold fury and in practised elegance, she strode away. Furious! because she had not been called to Brigand Olliot for THREE DAYS! He had sworn to her that she would attend him in his patronly duties at least every other day at the inner courtyard of the Ice Palace. Only here in this forsaken wasteland was there natural sunlight and warmth, the finest of food and wines, lackeys to fawn and fall to her every whim and... her Olliot. Her Olly, handsome, witty, strong, manly (she told him so, often), powerful and rich.

If only, if only he was all of that... and not merely powerful and rich!

Still, she had 'made her couch' as the old proverb rang and she only had to share it temporarily with six other Ladies, ah no, only five now, since that unfortunate 'infection' last week had taken Lady Ciprilla le Courtney conveniently out of the way. It had been her Kin-Aunt Skaggerack's wise counsel and trusted family jeweller, that had enabled her to smuggle-in three doses of Wolfbane-Root extract in her Keltik Tiara. Only two more 'accidents', plus a recurrence of that mysterious and pernicious 'infection' to arrange, until she achieved her dream... Wife to Brigand Olliot and his grieving widow Briganne de Dybrovnik, not too long thereafter!

The Lady Crimson de Dybrovnik stood and admired herself in the ancient ebony and tourmaline mirror of her outer chamber. Long braided hair of luminescent algae-green hue, a sharp and fine nose, like the prow of an ice-breaker galleon, eyes of a deeper blue than even the salt-pools of the Royal Western Spas and a figure that could 'knock a man dead'. Two in fact... so far.

To the left and right of the mirror were two of the Tapests that she owned. She had worked so hard for the five that she now had, two more even than Gannymede Mau-Mau, the sixth and last Lady brought to Olliot for his selection as wife. Beautiful she was too, Crimson had to admit... for the moment.

Her sister-in-kin Aelen had bequeathed to her the first and finest Tapest that she had ever seen. Their kin-mother Shannon was the most beautiful woman ever and the centre-piece of that Tapest. It flowed, pulsing with light and colours, shapes, scents and sounds that defied description. Her kin-mother Shannon could put her hand inside it, to secrete small items there for safe keeping, invisible and un-gettable by anyone else. What secrets and precious things still lay there, three years after her death, she wondered? A small tear escaped her otherwise steely eyes.

A loom-maiden quartet had been especially abducted

to create that Tapest for her mother and, to ensure its complete integrity, all had afterwards been executed and interred with high honours. All except one unfortunately, who had mysteriously escaped and still eluded capture.

Her own Tapests were (unlike those of her mother and sisters), the result of barter and war and as such, she could not place her hand inside any Tapest to find what had been hidden... what a frustration! She wondered if Aelen had found what their mother had discovered and secreted.

She longed for her very own Tapest to arrive, today maybe? She'd willingly given half of her hair to be woven into... whatever it was that they wove with. That would make it HER Tapest, hers to use in whatever way she could. Those lazy loom-rats below were so slow and unreliable! That thought brightened her features. She could then place her own secrets and valuables there and... perhaps the legends were true. That somewhere inside for only the 'worthy' to find, was something precious. Hidden somehow, somewhere within, a thing so precious that even the Loom-girls knew not of its existence. Her own kin-mother Shannon had intimated that she had finally (after years of searching and reflection) found that thing of great value just days before she had collapsed and died of Cold-fever. Aelen also was now dead, assassinated by a rival clan assassin. She paused and lowered her head briefly in remembrance and respect to kin-sister and mother.

Then, as taught to her by her kin-mother, having gazed

upon this Tapest, she now turned on her heel and put her back to it, to reflect… to try to see! Dimly in her mind she saw patterns, worlds and comets in motion, strange words and symbols but again felt… nothing. Why nothing? Her kin-mother and kin-sister had both said that they felt… something. She tried to convince herself though, that she saw a little more every time that she tried.

Turning, disappointed again, she reviewed her five Tapests. Three cities had fallen at the cost of countless lives taken and given by her Guards and Sammury, for her to have these precious items for herself. Her fawning commanders-militant to the north (keen for their own advancement and profit) awaited the news of her elevation as kin-wife to Brigand Olliot and now held three stockades of Guards and Sammury at her disposal.

Turning, she saw the old 'Legends, Insights and Meditation book of the Sages' that she had been given as a child by her Kin-Aunt Skaggerak. She kept it at the side of her sleeping couch. Odd that it lay open… on the chest next to the Tapests.

I must have put it there last night, she wondered, in case the Brigand should call?

Brigand Olliot having now returned to her thoughts, she decided she must see to her plans that must surely be executed today. Her long and elegant stride quickly took her to the courting-couch and she sat on the elk-skin covered white marble dais by the blazing fire-hearth. She idly turned a few pages of the Insights book on the ancient oak chest which held her wines and Keltik Tiara.

Pausing briefly, she considered should she (as advised by her kin-mother and kin-sister) daily read and meditate upon a portion of those archaic writings of the sages? No! She had important things to do today. Snapping the book closed and placing it by her side, she opened the trunk and took her Keltik Tiara in her hand. Important work there was indeed to do today!

Striding out once again, to where her serving-girls held dresses and scarves for her approval, her long legs made her silken gossamer underskirts rustle. She placed the Tiara at a jaunty, yet stylish angle on her head and... the ground beneath her feet shook and heaved! Loud bangs and grinding, graunching sounds filled the air; she struggled to stay upright and reeled about the floor.

More very loud bangs and their echoes continued to reverberate through the caverns, corridors, halls and apartments of Atoll Dubh for several seconds. Cries and oaths came from below and all around. Red and blue dust from neglected chandeliers above swirled down upon her head, littering her fine bodice-gown and waistcoat. With a sharp intake of breath and not a thought for her maidens and lackeys behind, she flung open her doors and ran, ran like the wind, to her Olly; her Keltik Tiara clattered unheeded on the floor behind her.

Pushing aside servants and even a couple of Black Guards in her haste, she finally entered the inner courtyard through a partially collapsed wall, the ornate swinging doors jammed shut at an alarming angle. Huge carved columns had fallen, chandeliers lay shattered on the floor but mercifully most of the ancient structure, hanging tapestries and furniture was intact. Brigand Olliot was staring fixedly at one fallen column and... weeping. As she opened her mouth to speak, Crimson saw what he was gazing at. A long, lovely, jet-black arm and hand with two cobalt wristbands and rings protruded from under the granite column. Zuu-Wendeley Longshanks!

"Oh, nooo, I liked her!" escaped her lips.

"She saw the column falling and tried... tried... she tried to push Gannymede away... but... too late... both of them..." so saying as his voice broke, Brigand Olliot turned and walked away slowly into his private chamber.

Time stood still for a while as she gazed at the fallen column and that once so beautiful and animated arm.

"Dear Zuu-Wendeley..." she said quietly to herself, "...of all of you, you only made any attempt at a friendship... oh well, at least now I don't have to..."

A squarky high-pitched voice startled her. "So, Crimmy! Less competition now for those of you left!"

This totally interrupted her train of thought.

The Lady Sula Sula McGootch was glaring at her. "...but you don't have to worry about me none neither; that so-called Brigand has made it perfectly clear that I'm not of interest. I'm leaving this forsaken smoky-hole on the next transport. I don't care if I have to endure the turgid 'conversation' of Black Guards, Sammury and Orient-Mariners for the next month; I'm going home!"

Turning on her heel, she stalked off, stepping over debris and cushions as if they didn't exist.

Only three then now to go, Crimson mouthed silently to herself, not realising that Brigand Olliot had been observing her closely through the one-way mirror of his chamber.

An accomplished lip-reader, he smiled through his now-dry tears at her words and the way that she stood, erect and poised… ready for anything.

"Now that's the kind of woman I want by my side." A movement and stifled groan to his left distracted him. A short, balding and rather fat man was struggling to rise from beneath a pile of fallen timbers. Centuries of dust obscured his remaining faded ginger hair, silken tabard and gaudy red pantaloons.

"Typical of you to survive!" Olliot spat at him. He heard Crimson outside shouting at the guards to "…leave the dead, secure the Hall and look to your master!"

His mind finally made up, he threw open his chamber door and walked imperiously up onto the ice-court colonnade, motioning to the approaching Black Guards to stay where they were. Taking a deep breath, he shouted to the milling, confused crowd below. "GUARDS! Round up every servant, lackey and slave and get this mess cleared up… IMMEDIATELY! LORD NESBITT! Break out the Brown Pioneer Guards in reserve and have them stabilise this Hall. Then conduct a review of every cavern, corridor and hall. Take Black Guard Zhula and empower her to clear all of the Lady's apartments, and put all but Lady Crimson de Dybrovnik's possessions into their travel chests and send all but her home, with all due despatch and speed. Let none of them re-enter their apartments." He stared fixedly at Nesbitt, who (getting the drift of his master's thought) nodded and bowed, dust falling from his balding pate.

Crimson's jaw dropped open and briefly she could not believe the implication. Wiping her mouth and pushing a dust-covered braid of hair from her face, she said (with as much demeanour as she could muster), "Oll... err Brigand Olliot, Master and Patron of Atoll Dubh, are you... aah, taking me to... to WIFE?"

"Come to me, Kin-Wife, Lady Crimson de Dybrovnik..." He smiled a big, beaming smile at her, looking now almost handsome. "I shall take you to wife. Come to me now, in full confidence and love."

As she ran to him and let him embrace her, her mind raced and she rejoiced in her heart to something, a force or whatever, that had opened to her the door to power, wealth and security. Wife to the Brigand, confidante to Regents and Commanders.

I do hope that the wedding isn't going to be here, she pleaded silently, that being her immediate and most passionate desire!

Nesbitt, still shaken, bruised and feeling very lucky not also to lie under that fallen column with Gannymede and Wendy (with whom he had lately been flirting), shook dust from his hair and bent to his tasks. He rubbed the back of his neck again. What he called 'My warning-itch' had started just before the earthquake which is why he'd walked very quickly away from the two ladies towards his own quarters. With not a little trepidation, he called to a tall, powerful and intimidating female Black Guard. "Zhula! Come here and delay not in compliance to my will."

She ran forward briskly and slammed to attention right inside his 'comfort-zone'. They would have been practically nose-to-nose if she had not been a full ten inches taller than he. Leaning back slightly, squaring his shoulders and trying not to react to the sweaty, oily, stench of her body-odour, he repeated, word-for-word, the Brigand's instruction, adding in a whisper, "...during your task, conduct a detailed search of their apartments... look specifically for poisons!"

Black Guard Zhula grinned and snapped her teeth together in obedience, as was the custom of the Guards. The sharp 'clack!' of her teeth always made Nesbitt jump. She stomped away, causing the timber floor to creak and tremble.

That is one mean and dangerous woman... female... thing... whatever... he thought to himself, *and should she actually find poison, I may well try it out on her...*

"NESBITT!" Brigand Olliot shouted. "Leave the guard to her duties. I shall escort my fiancée away from this dust and mess! Send to the kitchens. We shall eat venison, fir-apple potatoes and asparagus with Solent-herb butter dressing by the hearth-fire. Go to my private quarters and bring a bottle of the '92 Champagne. We shall be drinking from my finest Orient-Gold goblets tonight!" He then picked up a big fur and casting it around them both, led her outside past another Black Guard, who saluted and shivered in the draught.

Outside, he turned, pointed and said, "Brown Guard Tholoss, bring that Tapest to us outside… carry it very carefully!"

Gretchen's latest Tapest, depicting the Lady Crimson de Dybrovnik, delivered less than an hour before to the Brigand Olliot, stood temporarily forgotten and neglected on a couch by the door. Falling debris and dust had had no effect upon it. Every curtain, chair, surface and even the Brown Guard were somehow irradiated by the Tapest. The background to the beautiful Lady Crimson de Dybrovnik was antique, atmospheric, deeply wrought in its textures and was vibrant… living! An iridescent ocean fed by a silver river, its port-city mansions, cliffs and mountains framed and wrapped around the woman whose beauty was so well sculpted. A forest with fruit trees lay to one side. Reflections sparkled on every living thing in the room and only a close observer would have noticed two similarly remarkable things. These were, movements on the lips and eyes of another fine lady depicted deep in the background almost invisible in the forest and having a marked similarity to Gretchen herself, minus her scars.

So far, no one had time to look and now Olliot and a delighted Crimson stood gazing, impressed and rapt at her exquisite new Tapest. They had no idea of what lay within, or what role that exquisite Tapest would play in their future.

Nesbitt meanwhile, having by now regained most of his composure, sent Blue Guard Simliss to re-awaken the Pioneer Brown Guards from their sleep-rest in the lower garrison caverns and stepped over the carnage and debris to his own couch, where his valise and order-manifests lay. Writing swiftly in Guardenese, the only language that the guards could read (no words longer than five letters), he quickly sent five order-manifests to the relevant Sammury and Guard-commanders and then picked his way through yet more debris towards Olliot's private quarters.

Olliot with his radiant bride-to-be on his arm, walked slowly in the outer ice court. It was freezing-cold but neither seemed to notice. Both then stood by the blazing fire-hearth, the mists and sea-breezes of little interest as they talked and laughed together.

I'd give a Tapest or two, to know what those two are hatching! Nesbitt thought to himself as he stepped over fallen timbers and rubble. He patted the very full gold-pouch on his belt, next to his two poison daggers, then scratched his back with his pen.

A league out to sea, an old small volcano-islet smoked anew and sent glowing red lava into an ocean that seemed to boil blue-black. A few small sparks from the eruption could just be seen. The two lovers saw nothing of this.

In the Forge, Weapons and Metal-Working Caverns below, damage was slight but there were huge amounts of dust still swirling in the warm fetid air. The Northern-Terran Engineer-Supervisor was counting his worker-force. Twenty-five... all present and able to walk... he was very relieved. They were counted as mere slaves, to the Brigand and the Sammury but not to him; they were his people. One and all of them were making sure that the forges were quenched and all machinery and tasks-in-hand were safely shut down. Hot steam from the volcanic vents and the boiling water that flowed along next to the finishing benches were never predictable but were the only source of power for the machinery. The occasional earthquakes and eruptions had caused many injuries and delays in the past. His workers were dealing with the mess very well... this was after all, not an uncommon occurrence.

Dust and soot obscured the burns and scars on the Engineer-Supervisors face and hands but his green and blue eyes shone bright below his long braided red hair. He walked over to the senior Black Guard and shouted, "Take half your Guards outside and check all sea perimeters and the tidal shore defences, then and only if there are no breaches, go on up and report to Black Guard Zhula in the upper Palace. Confirm also that I am securing all forges, workplaces and materials. There are no serious injuries and full production will re-commence at the next rotation, after I ensure that no damage to forges or machinery have occurred."

"You have no authority over me, Supervisor-Engineer..." the Black Guard spat out "...I am..."

"UNDER MY AEGIS and at my displeasure and

word, subject to the full discipline of trial by combat. I'm sure you recall what happened the last time one of your kind disobeyed me." He nodded to the corpse of a Black Guard nailed to the wall by the door.

The Black Guard glanced over that way, grimaced and then snapped to attention, clacked his teeth and scowling, turned and called to his Guards to, "FALL IN!"

Thick as two short planks, thought the Engineer-Supervisor as the Guards jumped.

A small man, missing his left hand from an old injury limped over and coughed politely behind the Engineer-Supervisor. He turned to face him. "Dat wus ane of t' wurst blow-outs oi'd say as but we's alright, right enough… oi've capped a new steam-ole an' there's plenty more pressure for us lathes and t' like."

"Thank you indeed, good master Seamus, and there's something more that you can do, once that half-cohort of Guards has gone. Take all our people to their cots and issue a pint of cider, ice and bread to one and all. I'll join you shortly."

"Dat oi will!"

The Engineer-Supervisor watched him go and, taking a deep breath, squared his shoulders as he watched the Black Guard lead a half-cohort outside. Was this really what he should be doing? Was there an end… a good end in sight to all of this?

In the upper Palace, some semblance of order was being regained. Nesbitt, by courtesy of the labours of the Guards and servants, was now able to make his way easily across an undamaged section of the green and amber slate floor. Passing through the Brigand's chambers, he unlocked the cellar door and again scratched the back of his neck. Down the stairs he went with a lighted ox-fat candle and drew two large demijohns of the '92 Champagne from the racks and put them onto the floor, wiping them free of that cursed red dust… red dust everywhere.

"One for them and one for me and my addled nerves," he muttered, scratching both his back and his neck.

A movement of colours close by caught his eye. He spun around and drew his knives almost without thought. In classic 'parry-stance' he crouched, rigid but eyes and ears scanning, searching, trying to feel… He stared, turned and turned again but could find nothing.

"That's the fifth time this fortnight that I thought I'd seen a blasted Ghecko… and now this earthquake and now this… itch… I just can't seem to scratch, just like after we lost that Patrol of Sammury at the old Hesperance Fortress." His spoken thoughts only making him more uneasy, he carefully sheathed his poisoned daggers and then walked with difficulty now, back up the stairs with a demijohn of Champagne under each arm.

Back in the Brigand's apartments, he looked out through the one foot thick, quartz windows and stared beyond the two figures outside at rising plumes of smoke in the far distance. The Tapest with them seemed to pulse with colours that made his eyes weep, or was it just the dust?

Again, that blasted itch! He scratched the back of

his neck. "Volcanoes now! Earthquakes and Gheckos, whatever next?" He shivered at the thought.

Below in the Loom-cavern, dealing with her girls and the panicking Blue-Guards, Gretchen had a pretty good idea of what that was going to be.

5. Messages and Memories

"I got a message from Gretchen not much more than two months ago," the Captain said as he pointed his old sea-knife at the ocean chart on the wall on the back wall. "A bird brought word to me but I was… errmm… delayed and I…"

"A bird spoke to you?" interrupted Grynne.

"Aha, no… no my lad, a Blue Ocean Hawk fetched up at the Admiralty and they sent and brought me out of pris… out of pris… out of errmm… well… Stap me Vittles, I can tell you, young master Grynne, my friend…"

Grynne beamed at that.

"…yes well, I was in prison at the time."

Grynne didn't look very surprised, as up to now, he was by no means sure that the Captain wasn't in fact, a Pirate!

"Nothing serious, you understand. A misunderstanding… that's all it was really, just a minor disagreement with a Major of the Humdeefs, over a comment I made. A mere observation as to the similarity of his face with the hull of an old sea-barge, that was being cleaned up outside the tavern where I was eating that day."

"This err, disagreement…" queried Grynne. "This disagreement didn't by chance involve any… swordplay, now did it?" he asked with the merest hint of a smile.

The Captain seemed to be staring idly at a stain on the ceiling of the cabin. "Hardly any to speak of… no…

no… not really," he said, trying hard not to laugh. He permitted himself a smile, as if to savour the memory.

Two Soldiers of the Major's Honour Guard laid out cold by a single blow of his right fist. Two more sent packing with their breeches around their heels, their swords spun out of their hands by a double-riposte with two table knives! Best of all, that portly, over-bearing, clumsy, ignorant, arrogant, blustering oaf of an excuse for a drummer-boy, so-called Major, pinned to the wall by the waistcoat with his own rapier. The Captain's eyes shone and his smile fairly beamed.

"No lad, the errmm, disagreement passed almost without incident and we parted on cordial enough terms. It was the Watchman that they sent to arrest me that caused the most rumpus. Fifteen men was quite too much on a full stomach and I didn't want the Old White Swan Tavern all smashed up. The publican Emily and I were… still are, best of friends. No lad, the soldiers rather enjoyed being pitted against a superior… I fancy… most of them didn't need very much medical attention and they were discharged from the military hospital on the same day… mostly… I hear that they made old barnacle-face a General when he got out of hospital. General Limestead-Fortesque to be precise. 'General Limp', the Humdeefs call him… behind his back, of course!" Now he let rip. A long, hearty laugh that led to a coughing fit and he leaned against the wall with his free hand, whilst he wiped his eyes with the back of the hand that held his knife, and drained the last of his ale from an old pewter tankard.

"Watch yourself with that knife!" spluttered Grynne, for he too laughed loud and long.

"Knife? Oh yes… hee hee hee… harrumph, yes… now, where were we?" The Captain steadied himself and pointed at the lowest part of his old battle-sea-chart. Opening his mouth, he scratched at his eye-patch and began to speak, but Grynne interrupted.

"What was prison like?" he asked, fascinated again, by the life and experiences of this Captain Witherspoon-Golightly.

"What? Oh… prison. It was quite a nice… change, to be honest. The Jailor was Thomas, one of the seven that made it back from the massacre at the Fortress. He looked after me right well. A fine cook he is, he'd been the cook on the Talon." He went silent for just a second or two. "Aye… we even had the 'Gentlemen Harpsichord and String Quartet' come and give a recital in the courtyard on Shrove-Tuesday. I paid for that, gladly. Better than the stinking lodgings I'd had in the town to be sure. Far better."

His eye caught the battle-chart. "You know, lad… the One has surprised me more than a dozen times with a providence wrapped up in a problem. What a thing is providence! Who'd have thought I needed time in prison so that Blue Ocean Hawk could come… who'd have thought… Now… to the business of seamanship and of battle!" His eyes gleamed as he gesticulated with the knife, growing taller somehow; he squared his shoulders as if for battle, right there and then.

"Atoll Dubh. No one at the Admiralty could make head nor tail of it or knew what to make of the message when they took it off the Hawk. It had my name, 'Atoll Dubh', 'Sogon' and 'Gretchen' and that was it, apart from some numbers. None of it made any sense to those gin-soaked dry-dock-rats but I knew, knew right then, that the legends and myths had to be true. Knew that Gretchen had been right all along. The numbers were the thing of course..." he said, nodding to Grynne, who out of politeness, nodded politely back. "...aye, the numbers. Navigation was never Gretchen's strongest skill, but she remembered more than enough of what I taught her."

"You taught Gretchen? Taught her when? and what? And is she in trouble and how do you know and how will we get there (wherever 'there' is) and how will we...?" Grynne had now interrupted the Captain one time too many.

"AVAST AND BELAY THERE, LANDLUBBER!" The Captain's bellow was ear splitting. "I've allowed you some leeway, my young friend, but what we're about here is dangerous and hard work. Stormy seas with treacherous tides and currents. Men and women who'd as soon split you in half as cut themselves a sandwich. We're at war, good master Grynne. At war, I say, the OLD WAR. It never ended, although some live as if it had... yet more as if it never had! I'll teach you my ways, the ways of the sea and warfare; for that is what we are about. Now listen and listen well." The Captain had slowly advanced on Grynne, with every step his voice becoming softer, but with gravity and earnestness. He pointed with his knife at Grynne's forehead.

Grynne strained back as far as he could in his chair.

"That brain of yours, that there fine young brain, I have to fill with knowledge. I can't be a doing that, if you keep interrupting. Now can I?"

The knife was now less than an inch from his forehead. He couldn't nod and through a dry throat he managed to whisper, "Yes, errmm… no… I mean… yes I see your, your, point," Grynne said as he stared fixedly at the knife.

"Hmm? Point? Oh yes… sorry about that, lad… but good, good." The knife was now withdrawn a safer distance from Grynne's forehead, as the Captain spoke on, but he still emphasised his 'points', with short, stabbing movements. He turned and walked back to the chart on the wall. "Those numbers were numbers of Latitude and Bearings. I spent some time (best part of a week in fact) at the Admiralty Chart Room and made myself some new charts. I'd never been happy with what the oceanographers had guessed was and wasn't there. Yes, guessed!"

Grynne looked shocked. Up until then, he'd assumed that all maps and charts could be trusted to be completely accurate. Gretchen had never said otherwise during her lessons.

"They claimed otherwise, those dunderhead scribblers and dry-land oceanographers," continued the Captain, "but they'd neither believed, nor recorded, what the legends and myths had indicated lay to the far south.

When I'd done me charts, I errmm, borrowed a supply ship that the Admiralty clearly had no... err plans to use in the... errmm... immediate future and a small crew. Superstitious bilge rats, one and all. Almost useless they were, unless led by the cudgel, sword and pistol. One of them actually said to me that," and he affected an accent, "...'we's none to 'appy 'bout t'old ship's cat... old 'Jinx'... name's unlucky as ship's carpenter 'as jist died of a fever, turned 'im ginger all over an' the cat bein' ginger too....' I told them to get another cat but they never did. I took old Jinx to Thomas at the jail, gave him a guinea too and bade him look after the old moggy. Anyhow, I told them that we were bound out to raid some old port-town in the west, promised them booty and rum. I knew they'd jump ship when they found out where I was really headed, so I didn't tell them till two weeks ago. I let them take one of the Cleveland's Tenders (every frigate of that class carries two small boats, 'Tenders', young Grynne) and last I saw, they were headed for the Seaward Islands. They may yet make shallow-sea-bed-oysterhaulers!" He laughed and shook his head at the memory of that ramshackle bunch of sea-flotsam that had briefly been his crew. "NOW! There be stories, tale-songs and there be legends about the Atoll," said the Captain. "Now then there's a thing! Do ye know the difference between a story and a legend?" he asked, with a glimmer of a smile on his face.

"Well, a legend is all fancy, whereas story... it's a fact. I suppose, errmm, yes, I suppose so."

"Supposition is a poor friend and a bad tutor, young Grynne. Deductions! Them's what gets a man into and out of trouble right properly. Suppositions now, they just get you so deep into trouble that you flounder. Don't give me that look of a par-broiled cat-fish, my lad, of course a man sometimes has to get himself into trouble, so that he can get others out of trouble but he has to have plans and ways and means of getting out of trouble. That's what deductions is all for. And deductions oft-times comes from knowing the difference between a story and a legend. Now, you take a look at what you think you know well. Just you look at them prints on your walls." He waved his hand magisterially and pointed to the many old hand-bills, labels and advertisements that were pasted to the walls, keeping the draughts out or just because of their nice colours and pictures.

As Grynne's eyes followed the Captain's hand, he noticed that as the old Captain got into the swing of his yarning, that his language and tone took on a different hue. The old sea dog now quite eclipsed the gentleman.

"Now those prints there, some of them is labels and adverts of what's in tins and jars and they sez what is definitely a fact! Them tins and jar labels, am I right?"

Grynne nodded.

"No, they isn't!! How often has there been only juice, or only a dried up festered old thing of a whatsit inside one of them jars or tins?"

"More often than there should be, I'll allow," Grynne confirmed and nodded. He had often been disappointed

79

to find mostly juice inside a tin, instead of the meat or vegetables advertised.

"Now them other handbills on your walls, they tell of a politician's talk…" As he spoke the name 'politicians', his face twisted in disgust. "…what is definitely the right way to steer a country, not a ship. Now, do you trust such a thing, or to say, would you trust such a man?"

Grynne shook his head. Gretchen had told him many tales of politicians, and he wouldn't trust a politician any farther than he could throw one. Which admittedly in Grynne's case, was about thirty feet.

"Rightly said, rightly said, master Grynne, and with such an elegant shake of your head. But now then, sometimes by accident or design, such a man (a politician) is right, or would have been right, if the people had have trusted him aright. So then, some things are more like legends that could never have been, or might have been!" said the Captain triumphantly.

"Errmm, yes… yes, I think I see that now," fibbed Grynne as convincingly as he could.

"What then… but by chance, a story gets to be song, then a fable, then a story again, and by chance or by providence, the truth bobs back up to the surface, sometimes like, like a returning tide. Sometimes a friendly wind takes such a thing, a song such as you'd sing, a legend perhaps, a scrap of a thing, an old parchment maybe, a scribbled thing…" he said, patting his vest pocket in a strange manner, "and it's as true a guide to your purpose of destination, as a new Admiralty chart with the ink on it, still wet." He patted his vest again and almost unbuttoned the pocket, but thinking better of it, he looked into Grynne's baffled face and laughed! "Haaaa Septacaemic Sea Serpents, did I really say all of that, just to get me to the point?! HA HA HA HA."

Once again, the two new friends fairly rocked and rolled with laughter at the Captain's lengthy verbosity. After a while, both men took deep breaths and looked a little more solemn… they were after all, talking of war.

"Well now, every bearing on that scrap of a parchment from Gretchen (sewn in her own fair hand), I take as true, as it fits the legends and such like as I know. And now here I am about to follow those same charts. I allow that I trusted an older chart too well and fetched-up on the shore of your 'False Bay'. Drat Island is aptly named to be sure! Fancy there being a shallow beach of pale blue sand! But that was a providence that only The One could have provided." He walked back over to Grynne and clasped his shoulder so firmly that it was almost violent, but with such deep affection. "Good master Grynne, what a providence and delight you are!" His eyes glistened and he turned away.

Grynne hardly knew what to say, so he wisely waited till the Captain wheeled around and spoke again. "Atoll Dubh is where Gretchen is. It's a place of volcanoes and whirlpools that can suck a tall ship to the bottom. Boiling seas surround it but ice flows and bergs of white spattered with red and lime-green ash make navigation no easy feat. Strangely, it seems to be that the sea-bottom thereabouts is a mere three fathoms… still enough to drown a crew, mind you! That's from one of the tale-songs I spoke of before… one that I trust. There's a fortress there of sorts, and underground, maybe below sea-level, caverns of industries. Trades of iron, wood and leather and a place of despicable dark-arts where beings like men are made, bred for labour and war they say."

"MADE! Like men! Bred…" Grynne was astonished and appalled. "They can do things like that? May the One have mercy!"

"Well said, my young friend, that and many another things of song and story remain to be seen… remains for us to both see and deal with. Admiree Sogon must somehow have known of Atoll Dubh from traders and whalers and I believe that Sogon established the Atoll as his base after he first took Louis the Unlucky's Fortress from us. After two major but unsuccessful land-wars, he disappeared for just over a year and then appeared back in his own lands and sent ambassadors to negotiate a peace. There was all kinds of talk and rumours as to what he was up to but few believed what I now know to be true.

As for Gretchen… well bless her little cotton-socks, only knowledge of deep peril and a loving concern for others could have taken her there. To achieve her rescue and to put a final end to Sogon's plans, we'll need help of course, a lot of help. Another two ships, Frigates of the Line, Warships they'll be."

Grynne looked astonished. "But where can we find such things?"

"WE! That's a right fine thing to hear from you, young Grynne. Yes, we will find such, at the farthest outpost of the Admiralty. A strange place it is too, stranger than even the Admiralty knows! That however is another story and you'll soon see for yourself."

Grynne fairly beamed at the thought of he and the Captain being a 'We' and his face flushed, as he anticipated the coming voyage to that 'Admiralty' outpost.

The Captain continued. "One of the Seven who returned with me is the Fleet-Captain at 'Admiralty Atoll'. A shore-garrison it is with a small fleet, about a week's sail from here. Those isles are at the end of the whaling fleets' lanes. Over to the east they be. I doubt you've ever seen ships over to the east, have you?"

"No, only sometimes to the south and north."

The Captain nodded. "Yes, to the north makes sense. You lie well out of sight here and the good fishing grounds and the Mineral-Islands all lie along the favourable currents and winds to the north. You've been well hidden here. You say you've seen ships to the south though… hmmm."

The Captain paused and tapped the point of his knife against the end of his nose. Looking down to the ground, he stood stock-still for several moments. Suddenly he straightened and Grynne almost jumped.

"By mid-day…" he said almost to himself, "I'll have shown you all that lays on the sea charts, and checked your skill with compass and sextant and then we'll see how well you handle those swords and guns. You'll need to pack your kit and I'll give careful consideration to what you'll need. We'll need some vittles from your food stores and drinking water from your cisterns. I want to make way the following morning, as soon as we can re-float, stock up and re-rig the Cleveland."

Grynne waited several moments, as the Captain appeared to be going over things in his mind. Then he raised his hand.

The Captain smiled and said, "Aye lad, you have a question!"

"Captain, sir. I have fine swords and Gretchen showed me quite well, I think, how to use them. Aye and I've guns too and I've set them in as good an order as best as I know how. I've musket balls too… by the box-load… but I've not got one ounce of powder. No gunpowder has ever floated ashore."

"That…" laughed the Captain, "…is not a problem, laddie. The Cleveland is a fast resupply Gunpowder ship. That's exactly why I ermmm… borrowed her!"

Later that day, after a rather late lunch (due to Grynne mastering the finer points of navigation, interpreting the stars, clouds and wind as a mariner, not as a landsman), Grynne sat silently on the old driftwood bench outside his workshop. He stared straight ahead, not actually looking at anything, not even at the strange bird alighting in the Cyprian tree not fifty yards away, waiting its time when Grynne would be alone.

"What ails thee, lad?" said the Captain with a

snort. "You look like you're halfway around the world already!"

"Puzzling things over, I suppose. I often just puzzle things over. I see that you're getting the guns and swords ready to teach me how to be a... a warrior. I never really thought that I'd ever be killing... people, Terrans. Fishing and hunting animals for food I know about and I'm content with their place in the world and mine. We're 'All of one flesh,' say the Sages. I know that one day I'll be in the cold ground... or at the bottom of the ocean. I'm content, as I say... Gretchen told me all about the One and the way... I'm content since... since I know for certain... but killing men..." He fell silent.

"Aye, lad... all of life and our eternities are wrapped up in the tales of the One and his Folk... our kith and kin, and I suppose... deduce in fact, that Gretchen will have shared the tales very well with you... we'll... 'Chew the fat' as they say... on these things, the times, tales and tomorrows... as we make our way east."

The Captain let another minute pass as Grynne puzzled on, staring out to sea.

"Good lad, good lad, I never knew a truly dependable warrior who hadn't searched his soul long and hard on such things." The Captain regarded Grynne for a few moments longer and then said, "Stay here and puzzle... stay and listen awhile. I've a few things to set up by the shore."

So saying, he picked up some weapons and strode through the kitchen-garden to the steep path down and onto the beach. The day was fine, with a gentle breeze slowly picking up and making small waves on the sea. He stood still with his back to the surface wind and, looking up, noted that the higher winds blew clouds from his right to his left.

He smiled and nodded.

"Tomorrow will be a good sailing day!" said Benjamin to himself.

6. BIRDS AND BATTLE-PLAY

As the Captain, that is 'Benjamin' now at his insistence, made his way down to the beach humming a pump-shanty, Grynne took his vegetable basket down from the wall peg and put a small trowel into it. Time to collect some vegetables for their evening meal.

As he walked out to the kitchen-garden, he continued to puzzle and he did try to listen for the One. What he actually heard after a few minutes of 'silence', as the wind turned and twisted leaves in the trees and softly caressed the herbs and bushes in his garden, was a bird-song, a new bird-song. It was a beautiful day and Grynne thought that he had never seen his garden looking so beautiful before, yet he saw it every day and nothing had really changed… although everything had actually changed in some special, strange and slightly scary way.

Then that new bird-song spoke to him directly… personally!

The bird was very unusual. It had now alighted on a thick branch of the old mustard seed bush in his garden. As he watched, it stretched out a wing and preened with its small, sharply-curved beak. A beak so shiny that it glistened like diamonds would glisten, Grynne supposed. Grynne looked more closely and realised with a start, that underneath the wing it preened was another, longer wing folded back upon itself.

"Two sets of wings! Blow me down!" he said softly.

The bird turned towards him at that but its eyes seemed to sweep right past him, without actually seeing him at all. Its eyes were pale blue, like the rest of its dappled lower body and legs. Its upper feathers were a pattern of darker blue-greens that were so familiar to Grynne that he said so out loud, "The colours of the sea, as I see them from the cliff-tops and your lower body, little one, is as pale as the sky above. You must be nearly invisible in flight. A perfect hunter."

The idea that suddenly formed in his head was absurd but he knew, somehow he knew, as if he had been told, "Go take that bird in your hand."

He put down his basket quietly and moved towards the bird like a hunter, slowly, smoothly and not bobbing up and down, like most folk do as they walk. The bird ignored him and turned to preen its other wing. As Grynne drew near and within reach, it almost seemed to sigh and to settle. Grynne reached out very carefully and gently picked up the bird in his left hand, saying very softly, "You beautiful bird."

He raised the bird level to his breast.

The bird now turned its head and looking him straight in the eye… sang.

If its first song had been unusual, this one was fantastic. A symphony it was, like two or even three birds were singing with sublime angelic harmonies. Grynne knew that with all his talent at music, he would never be able to play or to whistle that tune. The bird was warm and comfortable in his hand and when its song came to a melodious completion, it rubbed its beak hard against Grynne's chest through the lacing of his blouse, then looked away towards the path.

"DON'T FRIGHT THAT BIRD!!" The Captain's voice though distant, was clearly in great earnest. A huffing and puffing sound preceded his arrival, all in a sweat, at the garden gate. Leaning heavily against the gate post and peering around the fencing laths, although pretty-well winded, he breathed as softly as he could manage, "Try not... to fright... that bird... that bird... young Grynne... that bird in... *your hand*!"

Grynne was treated to a rare sight. The Captain looking totally non-plussed!

Benjamin took in the scene. Grynne was standing by the mustard bush. With a Blue Ocean Hawk in his hand!

"Keel-haul I for a landlubber..." He walked over slowly and beamed at Grynne. "Blow me down, laddie, you're a blessing to be sure. Only one other man I know of has ever caught a Blue Ocean Hawk in his hand. That was me and I have to admit, the first time I tried the trick, it gave me quite a peck!"

Grynne was really enjoying the sensation of holding this beautiful, warm and soft and (so far) gentle bird, in his hands. "She seems quite happy. I've always dreamed of holding a beautiful raptor-bird like this in my hands."

"That's why she's so content, my lad. I was so nervous and clumsy when I did what you've just done, that I can't in all good conscience blame her for that... peck." He rubbed his hand, in painful remembrance.

The two men were both staring now in fond awe at the bird who, although not struggling, seemed to decide that things were not going speedily enough. It sang a short and rather sharp 'Trill' and looked Grynne straight in the eye.

The Captain cleared his throat and spoke. "There'll be a message tied to its leg. Pull the longest cord with a roundel-knot at the end, to release it."

Sure enough, there was the cord and Grynne pulled it, releasing a tightly-rolled, pale gossamer-thin sheet of skin. The bird shook itself.

Again, somehow Grynne just knew and feeling ever-so sad, said, "Can't you stay for just a little while longer, little one?"

The bird looked him coolly in the eye.

"No, she can't. She mustn't! Farewell, me fine beauty, fair winds, fine weather and good hunting be yours." The Captain spoke softly and lovingly to the bird.

Grynne opened his hand and the bird hopped up onto his shoulder and dug its talons into his flesh.

"Aaaa!" gasped Grynne.

The bird looked about itself both high and low and cocked her head towards Grynne. It gave a long rub of its beak against Grynne's brow, leaving an almost invisible smear of oil there and spreading its outer wings... leapt up into the air!

"Aaargh!" was Grynne's farewell to his little feathered-friend and he rubbed his bleeding shoulder gently. The two men watched as the bird climbed swiftly upwards, then catching a thermal current and spreading its inner, gliding-wings… simply disappeared!

"Wow…" breathed Grynne.

"Astonishing!" muttered the Captain.

"You're a fortunate man," said the Captain as he gripped Grynne's shoulder.

"Aaargh!"

"Oops, sorry Grynne! Normally only Sylphs can call and catch Blue Ocean Hawks."

"Sylphs?"

"Yes, Gretchen is a Sylph. Rare they are and beyond the ken of mortal men. Did you notice how she would talk to plants and to animals?"

"Yes… sometimes she made it seem that they spoke back to her, birds, fish in the sea and even trees."

"She could hear them, lad, and that's how she was able to send us that message. Give it here to me now, laddie." The Captain held out his hand and took the pale blue skin roll, which though gossamer-thin was as strong as strong could be. He stroked it for a second or two while he smiled and muttered softly to himself. "She made, she held this and not such a long time ago." Sniffing it once and smiling anew, he unrolled it.

Craning his head so that he too might see, Grynne demanded, "Well? Well? Well, what has she written?"

"But one word, but one word… 'SOON'! It's what she's sewn on it that's important… important? It's VITAL! That's what it is" He stroked the fine needlework, smiled proudly and laughed. "Only she could have done this."

He drew out the skin which was unbelievably nearly a foot square and covered with the most delicate and colourful sewing that Grynne had ever seen.

"It's, it's a map and a plan, plans even, of a place and it has depth."

"Yes, laddie, this is Tapest sewing, look from different angles and you see one part of a building on top, or below another level. This... this thing of beauty will help us breach Atoll Dubh's defences and save lives, our own, our comrades and that of many innocent Terrans too."

"Comrades?" asked a puzzled Grynne.

"Yes... comrades, that we yet have to find and muster, young master Grynne. Soon, she wrote and so the times now come to a head and we must be moving!"

Once again, the Captain's eye swept over the embroidery and then he noticed a name hastily written in a small space on the edge.

"Nesbitt!" His face twisted in disgust. "That mankii-worm! With him there as well..."

"Who is Nesbitt?"

"A traitor, a thief and a maker of mischief beyond tell."

Alarmed now and very worried for his friend, pretty Gretchen, Grynne seemed to spring to attention. "So we must be on our way immediately!"

"Stand fast!!" said the Captain and gripped Grynne's undamaged shoulder this time. "...'more haste, less speed', as the old Sages said and they're right. There's preparations to make. Not the least being to test and to train you up in at least the rudiments of swordplay, gunnery and ballistics. We've provisions to pack, water-barrels to fill…"

"Wine barrels too!" interrupted Grynne.

"Wine, you've wine here?"

"Aye, not a lot but every now and then, a barrel or two of ale or wine washes ashore. I use it for cooking… mostly."

"Cooking… cooking! Laddie, you're a caution!"

"Some of the barrels are really sticky and the stuff inside them smells really strong. I put those in the sea-cave. I've never tried it… that reminds me… I was picking some herbs and vegetables for our meal." Grynne turned and, spotting his basket, walked to it and, pulling up some carrots and swede, added them to what he'd already collected and turned towards Benjamin.

The Captain grinned at him as they walked back and into the cabin. "Those… sticky barrels you've got… is there branded into the top-lids or the sides 'Jammakey', or similar?"

"Hmmm? Yes, yes, I'd guess that that's what's branded, right enough."

"Wonderful. Wonderful, they'll be rum barrels then and even if it's too old to drink, they'll make a right fiery acrid blaze when we attack the inner defences of the Atoll Dubh!"

The Captain fell silent for a moment and watched as Grynne washed the vegetables under a spout and then fell to the task of preparing vegetables from his garden for their next meal.

"Aye lad, we'll be working well into the night. Put that stew pot you're filling with garden-vittles into your fire-pit... with some of your wine and cover it well. By nightfall, it'll be nicely done and a fitting end to our day. Tomorrow I'll bring the Cleveland in myself between the Pinnacles at..." He paused and walked outside. He then wetted and held his finger up into the breeze, looked at the clouds, grunted and continued. "On a northerly wind at... high noon-tide and you can lower all of our Kit, Caboodle, Tackle and Tin onto the deck. Then you can dive down, and we'll be on our way."

"You can bring the Cleveland between the Pinnacles on your own! Blow me down! That will be something to see and yes, I've ropes and tackle long enough to lower... wait a minute... dive... dive... from that height! It's sixty feet... and more!"

"Well-aye laddie! You'll make the drop just fine and dandy. Just make sure it's your hands that break the surface... not that thick skull of yours!"

Dodging the knife that Grynne threw at him, the Captain laughed loudly. "Haaaa!" but stopped, as he viewed the blade, deeply embedded in the wooden doorframe at his side.

"Oh, I knew you'd dodge that... just fine and... dandy, my dear old Captain!" laughed Grynne.

"Ah yes... tis true enough... and less of the 'old', laddie... yes indeed, maybe I won't have to teach you all that much." The Captain stared at the knife. "When you've done, join me on the shore."

The time that they spent in the afternoon sun on the beach was just a blur to Grynne. Although he and Gretchen had sparred and duelled many times for fun, he had never actually fought with a sword before.

He learned swordplay on board the Cleveland, in and around the rigging and masts, then on hard rock, on soft sand, then standing on a floating pallet on the sea. The Captain had him jumping from rock-to-rock whilst whirling a cutlass and a long-knife in his hand. He cut, he slashed, he threw, he juggled sword and knife from hand-to-hand, as he ran backwards and forwards. He learned to move his entire body quickly from side to side. Backwards, sideways, every which way, he parried blow after blow from the Captain's swords, cudgels and spears. Using belaying pins, knives, tankards even, he held the Captain's attacks and suffered only a few bruises and two small cuts. All through that time, the Captain was his attacker, relentless he was. Old... hardly!

Looking down the barrels of the Captain's guns, he dodged shot after shot. Then it was his turn, trying to shoot the Captain and the rocks, coconuts and sticks that he threw into the air. Slowly, he improved. With the Captain loading, he emptied a whole gunny-box of musket balls and rifled-slugs. Two barrels of fine black-powder too, all emptied. The last five shots that he fired, split those five rocks into a thousand pieces.

The captain now leaned again a coconut palm, breathing deeply. Grynne had been told to take a swim, a long swim out to sea and when he heard the Captain's final pistol shot of that day, he was to swim back to shore. The Captain had also taken a swim earlier, hot and sweaty he was too, after all of that swordplay and gunnery. The salt water had taken away the acrid stench of gunpowder smoke out of his nostrils and he could now enjoy the scent of the palms, grasses and flowers on the shore.

Pointing at nothing (for the first time that day), the Captain fired his final shot into the air and re-loaded. Grynne turned, dove down deep like a dolphin and swam back to shore. Walking up from the shore, he wrapped a towel around his waist and sat down on the sand next to the Captain, who sat on an empty barrel and leant against the prow of the Cleveland.

Neither spoke for a while.

"So… will, will I make… a warrior, Captain? Can you make a warrior of me?"

With a broad grin, the Captain replied, "Ah, it'll not be me that makes you a warrior, Grynne me lad, but your adversaries! I've made you as good a fighter as I can. Warfare makes warriors." He regarded Grynne now with an unflinching eye. "I'm well impressed! A very fine fighter you are too and with a clear eye for a sure shot at the distances you'll need most. We'll practise with the Culverin breechloader cannon on the Cleveland as we travel. I see no likelihood that you'll do any less well with the heavy-ordnance guns than you have with rifle and musket. And it's about time you called me Ben. You've done me great respect as your Captain in so many ways… now's the time, my good friend Grynne. Call me Ben, from now on."

Blushing, he replied, "I… I… will, Ben! It'll take a while to break the habit, Capt… Ben, I mean."

"When we find ourselves a crew of sailors and take on Marines, you'll need to address me still as 'Captain' but when we're together, or at table, it'll be Ben. No, lad… I've never seen the like of you before. Quick to learn, fast, sharp as a razor and strong! I've heard of your kind before but never had the privilege…"

"My kind?" said Grynne, not at all sure whether to be flattered or offended.

"Aye laddie, you are of a noble and somewhat uncommon heritage but you've no knowledge of your parents or kin, as you told me last night. No knowledge of them at all, have you?"

Grynne shook his head.

"That knowledge will come soon enough. That's the good news, tis now the time to tell you the bad news."

For a few long seconds, Grynne did not know what to say. The events of the last two days, what he'd heard and felt, what he'd seen, the emotions stirred, both horrified and fired his heart… and the puzzles… the puzzles that were whirling in his mind, were now almost too much for him.

Ben spoke softly. "You'll lose your great strength the further away that you journey from this island. Grynne my dear soul, only your great strength held me off when we fought just now. I've not had to work so hard... just to keep my sword in play..." He gestured to two broken swords laid by on the nearby rocks. "...not had to work so hard... and I've never broken two swords in a day... I've only broken two, in two hundred and twenty years!"

Grynne was astonished. "You mean to say that I'm stronger than other folk, stronger than other Terrans? I never knew. I thought that everyone could... but... I'll get weak once I leave here?" He looked up and around at his island, up to Mortlocks mountain, to the tree terraces where the wheat grew and up to where his beloved cabin and garden lay concealed. A huge wave of loss all but consumed him. He was prepared to do anything to save pretty Gretchen and to take his place in the great scheme of things but now he realised for the first time that to go... he actually had to go... to leave his home and all that he had ever known. He would become weak... home was where his strength had come from. The concept puzzled and frightened him. How could this be? How could he be of use in a battle if he was to become weak? He desperately wanted Gretchen to be saved... how could he help her if everything that was of him, was to change? Could he be, could he remain, man enough for the task?

Ben remained silent as Grynne wrestled with things that he barely understood, if at all. Then the answers came to him as he heard again from his memory, the Captain's... Ben's words. 'Well impressed... never seen

the like… quick… sharp… a privilege… get weaker…
weaker not *weak*!'

He took a long and deep breath.

"Not *weak* but weaker than I am now… and I'm now
trained in combat!" he thought out loud.

"How long will it take us to get to this… Atoll Dubh?"
He now turned and looked Ben straight in the eye.

"All told… ermmm… winds being fair, our new charts
and Gretchen's information being accurate… the best part
of a month. It's not that far really but we have to make a
few… stops… to take on more supplies, warmer clothing,
crew, Marines and such like. Yes, my dear friend, you'll lose
some of your strength but you'll be at least as strong as
other lads, of your own age and build. It's your spirit that
will keep on growing, my lad, and it is the spirit of a man
that keeps him going through even the thickest of battles."

Grynne stood. "I'll go, I'll work hard, I'll learn as much
from you as I can. I think that I did know all along that
Drat Island couldn't be for all time, not for me. Blow
me down, I even wrote a song once called 'Not for all
time'. Gretchen really liked to hear…" A lump came
into his throat. Clearing that with a cough he continued,
"…Gretchen really liked that song and I'll cut my way
through whatever evil we find, to sing it for her once again!"

Ben embraced Grynne and hugged him hard. "Good
lad, fine lad, I knew, I just knew!"

Both laughed loud and long.

Ben looked out to sea and said, "Grynne my lad, how
far could you throw an old sea dog like me?"

"AAAAaaaaaaaaaaaaaaaaaaaaaaa."

Gu-DUNCH!

It was a good few seconds before the Captain's head broke the surface almost thirty feet out from shore. He blew sea water out from his moustache and gulped some air.

"Ha ha ha ha! That was grand!" He swam back to the rocks and as Grynne reached over (giggling) to haul him out, he spun, heaved and flipped Grynne head-over-heels into the water. Grynne turned on him in a flash and the Captain had to use all his tricks to withstand even Grynne's playful fighting.

"Hold, hold! That's enough for today, I'll be no use with a broken arm!"

"You tricked me, Capt… Ben!" laughed Grynne.

"Aye lad, and that's the last lesson for you to puzzle and ponder upon for today… and every tomorrow…" Ben was not laughing now. "Aye, lad, and our foes will trick you. They'll trick, bamboozle, distract, confuse, giggeryfall, set traps and use their foul and black demonic arts to waylay you. Listen well to every tale I tell, listen to and learn of the men that we'll be sailing with and fighting alongside. The most difficult thing (it's a sore temptation-riddled thing, mind you) is to learn to think like our adversaries, get into their foul minds, anticipate and expect their stratagems whilst still remaining… whilst still retaining your own good conscience… and a clean spirit… a good name before men is one thing… but to honour the ONE… in this old world…" Ben stood in the shallow water and looked out to sea neither smiling nor frowning.

The deep, the old, ancient cold deep was reflected in his face.

Turning, he said softly, "The sun is lauwerin', Grynne, and we have provisions to pack and... and, Stap me Vittles, is that what I think it is?" He glared at the straggly-looking bird flapping clumsily downwards into the terrace of trees below Grynne's cabin.

"Aye, that's an Orogoratory Bird, that is," replied Grynne, who was fast picking-up Ben's manner of speech.

"Is that what you'd call it here? Now, that wouldn't be Gretchen's naming of that feathered bit of avian treachery, would it? She'd a rare way with daft words!"

"Well, yes. She named it so to me. She also told me..." and he laughed, "...that she'd heard that they were once people. Terrans. Money-keepers and courtiers from a far-off land, she said. They then fell from favour with their masters and were transmogrified by the black arts of the Magi-Schienses and turned into those tatty-looking birds. I thought that quite funny and made a song up about it. I've found jewellery and all kinds of shiny objects and keys in their nests. They carry them in a kind of pouch on their stomachs. They don't fly very well at all... and only in good weather. I don't think that they'd taste too well either. I cooked one once when rations were low but the flesh was all stringy and oily and so I threw it away. Even the feathers turned rotten after a few days. No use at all... that ugly bird!"

"So… you didn't actually EAT one, not even a little bit?" Ben said, looking very serious.

"No… no why? There's no truth in the story… is there…? Oh my word!"

Ben was staring at the tree and nest where the bird had landed. Stroking his beard and surprised at how much water remained there, Ben wrang it out and dried his hands on his pantaloons that lay nearby. "You weren't to know and there was no errmm… harm done." He walked up onto the shore and then pulled on his pantaloons, boots and shirt. Checking a long rifled shotgun, he shouldered it, and picking up his powder and shot bandolier, turned again to Grynne who was looking a little pale and muttering, "Blow me down… I could've eaten…"

The Captain harumphed and said, "Get your kit together, Grynne, take what we don't need up to the cabin and stow the rest where I showed you in the Cleveland's hold." He took a few steps towards the trees, then stopped and turned again to Grynne. "I'll be brief, lad. These Courtier birds were treacherous and meanly spirited as the men and women they once were and remain much the same now. They can't talk but will nod and shake their heads when an Orient questions them. They hate Orients, they hate the northern peoples and all the Terrans of the continent and islands. They hate each other, and they hate life almost as much as they fear death. Neither neutral are they nor allied, but they'll cause, aid and abet whatever will cause grief, pain or sorrow whenever and wherever they can. They stole whilst men and women and they steal as yet. The jewellery and other stuff that you found is their way of pretending that they are still of value and control the coffers of the great emperors that they once served. Not exactly immortal as you'd say but they don't die naturally… and as you discovered, they're not invulnerable! If that flying scaby-serpentine wretch of a thing sees me, it'll be off and tapping on the window panes of Admiree Sogon's Battle-Barge like a flash and we'll lose our advantage of surprise. That flying rat dies here and now!" At that, he ran off at a trot… low and silently over to the tree line and disappeared.

Knowing well enough to make no move or sound himself, Grynne sat down on a barrel and waited.

Not a minute later there was a BANG! and a crashing thump. Ben's voice came from the trees. "All good, laddie! I'll see you up at the cabin. I've a nest to check!" He sounded well pleased.

What neither of them saw was another Courtier bird watching coldly from the far shore, in the shade of a fallen palm over a rockpool. Its broken wing was nearly healed now and as Grynne hoisted boxes and barrels up into the hold of the Cleveland, it continued to chomp on some jellyfish, barnacles and mussels from the rock-pool. Stretching her damaged wing painfully, she chattered and spat broken shells out onto the sand, her deep black eyes squinting into the falling sun, a plan forming in her bitter and eternally-disappointed heart.

Jumping down from the Cleveland into the warm, soft sand, Grynne put the few things that remained on the beach into his gunny-sack, hoisted it up onto his shoulders and set off towards the path. As he trudged, he reflected again on the astonishing and life-changing events of the last two days. Was it really only yesterday, an afternoon just like this (but nothing like this), when he had first met the Captain, his new friend Benjamin Witherspoon-Golightly? Ben, what a puzzle he was. The Cleveland, the Admiralty, Atoll Dubh, all puzzles. Gretchen imprisoned, somehow it would appear, imprisoned willingly! Courtier birds, Blue Ocean Hawks... one an ugly and the other one a beautiful puzzle!

Benjamin was to be sure, an honest, upright and dependable man and one to be trusted and followed cheerfully and with full confidence... but how did Grynne know that so surely and yet still puzzle over him?

"I wonder how OLD he actually is?" pondered Grynne aloud.

There was more than a hint of grey in his red hair and beard, he was strong and athletic to be sure and his sword skills were... Ben's words now came back to him, 'Swords... two broken... I've only broken two, in two hundred and twenty years!' he had said. Grynne knew from his books that most Terran males lived for 'three-score years and ten', seventy when all told. How could that be? Another puzzle!

As Grynne trudged back home and the Captain took keys and talismans from the dead Oragoratory Birds' nest, the bird's injured mate hopped quietly along the sand and up the gangplank of the Cleveland. She knew the layout of that 'Leda' class vessel well and shortly she had made her way clumsily down through the Midships Fore Hatchway and aft to the stairs down into the Orlop hold. The After Magazine, Fish and Spirit Rooms lay there and she found stale weevily bread and dried fish barrels open. Filling her pouch as full as she could, she made her way to the Shot Lockers which surround the Pump Shaft and Ships Well. There was seepage water there and enough space to conceal herself behind the racks of lead musket balls.

Settling down as well as she could, she painfully spread her damaged wing and, munching a small dried fish, plotted her revenge. Later she fell asleep and dreamt of her last meeting with Emperor-Admiree Sogon on his mist-concealed battle-barge, the Vengeance.

7. Feelings and Forebodings

Black Guard Zhula had bundled the remaining Ladies into a transport ship, with their belongings neatly packed (well, actually not all that neatly) and sent them away from the Pole-dock with suitable (though basic) provisions and wine, all in less than an hour. That transport was bound for Sogon's battle-barge with weapons and over two hundred new Guards. The Ladies' protests had been feeble and somewhat unconvincing, she thought. They looked as though they'd had the stuffing knocked out of them and just wanted to be away from what The Lady Sula Sula McGootch described as "…this unstable, smoke-filled gloomy, damned and dangerous place…" That sounded really odd to Zhula; she liked it fine here, just a bit more combat (or actually… a LOT more combat) and it would be just right!

Later, when carrying out the rest of her orders, as expected she had indeed sniffed-out poison. Wolf-bane poison. It was very well-concealed in a priceless gold, platinum and diamond encrusted Keltik Tiara. She was not surprised at whose head it adorned. She had informed Nesbitt without emotion and quickly withdrew. His smile boded well for her. She had acquitted herself professionally, secretively and in accord with his wishes. Zhula, in compliance with her orders had also retrieved what she could from the apartments of the Ladies and had collected the five Tapests that had been part-buried under the collapsed ceiling and walls of Lady Crimson de Dybrovnik's apartment. Oddly, they had suffered no damage and were not covered in red dust, like the rest of her things. She took special care to place them on an undamaged table close to the Brigand's room.

Above her, Nesbitt was now noisily supervising the re-building of the main Hall and repairs to much of the fortress and the caverns below. The Sea-Dock itself was untouched by the quake which was just as well, as two empty transports were expected within the next week and Zhula knew that the quotas of weapons and guards exported last month had been lower than The Emperor-Admiral had demanded. That was all she knew of the matter but she could see that the Brigand was concerned and had sent untrained Blue Guards to reinforce the Terran slave-workers in the breeding caverns. A risky stratagem in every way!

Three of Atoll Dubh's five whaling-ships lay on the far side of the quays and were now empty of their raw-materials for breeding more Guards. Zhula stared for a while, there was something at the back of her mind… but whatever it was she couldn't quite place it.

After completing and signing the last order-manifest, Zhula called the company of shipwrights, sailors and dockers to attention, stood them down and sent them to their quarters for a decent feast with cider! Alone now on the quayside, she took a deep breath and took the stairs to the upper stores at a run. Good exercise in this restricted place. One hundred and twenty steps, in less than a minute! She checked her breathing and counted her heart-beat. Hardly different than when on the quayside below. Excellent! Her next evaluation should put her ahead of the other Black Guards and in line for promotion to Sea-Commander. Seeing a crate of iron-ore destined for the furnace-ironworkers to her side, on the racking, she hoisted it to her shoulder and jogged along the corridor. Although the quake itself, the damage and death she had seen it cause, had not disturbed her in the least, nevertheless she felt on edge. Something was out-of-line, something wasn't in-line... what could possibly be wrong?

Later, walking by the Breeding-Cavern below the quays, where she and all her brother and sister Black Guards had been 'Made', she paused. Unsheathing and checking her weapons for rust, she stroked the smooth blades and leather-bound hafts, held the edges along a burning corridor torch to check for wear and remembered... something. The smells were the same, the sounds of the 'Newly Made' as they were called, the same... but yet? Had she been the product of a family as the Captain (and even Grynne) had been, she might have understood the feelings which lay dimly-perceived under her love of duty, orders, combat training, hard work, preparation for war... and there it was again... what was war? What for, who for, who was she/was it... what was it? There was doubt here, no fear, just...? She could not quite bring it to mind, no matter say it aloud, what on Terra was it?

What was all this about? A bell rang somewhere and back in her right mind now, she jogged along to her midweek battle-rounds.

The Lady Crimson de Dybrovnik was checking out her new chambers and inspecting her new maids-in-waiting and servitors. Her previous slave-girls and lackeys still lay under the collapsed ceiling at the rear of her former quarters. If they were all dead, it was unfortunate but of little actual consequence. Her new chambers were fine... fine... except for the dust, a fallen screen-wall and cracked quartz window overlooking the North Bay and tidal approaches. Her new maids-in-waiting seemed capable and very eager to please. Her husband-to-be was fussing about all over the place, and had washed, changed and... well... changed! As he had led her hand-in-hand through the Hall and out to the fire-hearth outside, his wry comments and flirting had made her laugh out loud twice! Instead of dragging his left foot slightly as he walked, he now strode like a champion and she'd swear that he was actually taller! Not possible obviously, but somehow...

"Crimson, my Dearest, come nearer to the fire and tell me what you think of this." His eyes twinkled and his lips were set in a beaming smile as he handed her the (almost transparent) gold Champagne goblet. Bubbles and sparkles of light from the heady liquor made her eyes widen and as he crossed his arm around hers and they both drank so very close together, his eyes seemed to glow.

"Ooo… the bubbles, they've gone… gone right up… AaaaaatishOOO!"

"You sneezed like a Tavern Ale-wench…" Olliot guffawed. "And you've not spilled a drop! Haa Haaaa!"

Playfully, she punched his free arm and giggled like a schoolgirl. "Ale-wench indeed!" Putting up her hand to her head, she realised that her Keltik Tiara was no longer there. "Bother!" She must have lost it but no matter. There was no remaining need for it. The next half hour flew by. Whilst she couldn't remember exactly all the detail amidst his revelation of great and complex plans, the confidences of military strategies plus the plots and machinations that explained his role in the great scheme of things, what was most amazing was how animated he was… how attractive… suddenly how manly and… yes… how… witty he had become! Could she actually… finally… be falling in love with this man?

Gretchen meanwhile had been very busy. She and Shelagh-no-tears had marshalled the Loom-girls, salvaged spilled dyes, re-strung hank-shelves and put everything back where it should be.

They had assessed which looms were undamaged or immediately repairable and had dealt with panicking Blue Guards whilst re-assuring a very pale and agitated Overseer Brack that "…all was well, the loom girls are all accounted for, full production will resume before the end of the day, your Guards are doing just fine (that was a total fib!) and yes, it IS necessary that I, Gretchen, check all the other caverns." That responsibility and the rank that went with it, she had earned over the last two years. She could go almost anywhere as she knew all of the trades but two.

Previously she had no need to enter the iron-foundry weapons and workshop caverns. The Terran Supervisor-Engineer there was well-spoken of, and replacement parts for looms and other items that she had ordered were of the highest quality. Also, the fact that he had had several attempts on his life by Black Guards (and none had survived) meant that he was probably a good man just looking after his worker-slaves. As for the breeding caverns, well... breeding the Guards in the Birthing Caverns was something that she had no desire to see and also... she might be recognised by one of the Maggii-Schience Terran Supervisors. It was just too great a risk.

Though never unexpected, this type of quake seemed to have done far more damage than any previous one. Usually a little dust fell and some doors would stick, or not close again.

Times are turning to Task! Gretchen thought... calling to mind that old proverb which more or less meant, 'Better wake up and do what you can do, right now!'

Her tour and inspection of the other caverns, their slaves, artisans and stores had been rapid and because of her knowledge of the corridors and passages, she'd managed to avoid the Black Guards as they marshalled the still drowsy Brown Guards to repair the damaged structures and walls... right up until she heard a voice shouting... that voice... Nesbitt! So he was here.

He must have arrived after I last met with the Brigand, she thought to herself, as his selection of prospective wives were shipped in. Typical! Just like him to arrive with a boat-load of aristocratic floozies.

The implications of that traitor being at Atoll Dubh, back once more in favour with the Admiral-Emperor, now occupied her mind and there was something else, something new and exciting. The other cavern that she had so far been unable to enter was the iron-forges and weapons cavern. This last quake and damage had finally given her access and she had seen in there several Terran slave-workers and a tall northern-man with a burned and scarred face, in the iron-proving section of the weapons-benches. He seemed to be totally in charge, which was most unusual;. Usually there would have been an Administrator Sammury over a senior Terran. Who *was* he and why was he there?

Gretchen walked right up to him and demanded, "Who... *exactly* are you and *why* are you here?"

He looked hard at her and placed his feet further apart, as if expecting attack. "You'll be the Loom-girl overseer. I've heard much of you... Gretchen... and all that to the good!" he smiled but did not relax until he bowed. "Forgive me... I am, madam, your servant Harry Bessler, former junior officer of the Crown at the Hesperance Fortress that once was and now by the grace of the One... Iron-Prover, Engineer-Supervisor and Quartermaster of Weaponry."

Gretchen actually gulped. "H... Harry... Harry *Bessler...* Hal?"

He stepped back as if struck. "Hal... it's been a *long time* since anyone called me Hal!"

Very quickly they told their tales. Ben and she had known each other well and over many years, she'd raised a very special child (not of her own clan), now full grown and very strong, on a remote island and they were now en-route with a small fleet. She had trained a small force of girls in combat on the Atoll and sent drawings plus other information to help the invasion.

Hal had been captured alive after the fortress at the Hesperance had fallen but was injured and badly-burned. He had been kept 'for sport' in the 'Pen' on the battle-barge Vengeance. Orient Emperors often held fights to the death between Guards, Sammury or prisoners, the survivor being rewarded with any new role of their choice, below that of Lieutenant Commander. For prisoners, the fight was 'rigged' and they were denied all food and given only water for five days before the contest. Hal had somehow managed to steal, save and secrete some rations and mercifully was the last prisoner to be called by which time, he had regained some strength.

He was matched in combat that day against a Sergeant Black Guard looking for promotion and around the Pen sat the Emperor and his senior commanders. He was given a wooden sword whilst the Black Guard chose her own weapon.

Surreptitiously, he had eaten his small cache of food but, feigning weakness, he appeared to stumble with one hand to the ground. As the Black Guard drew close and raised her axe for what she thought was going to be an easy kill, he hit her with his wooden sword in the throat. She fell, dropping her weapon and clutching her throat and he had then… well… he had then beaten her un-fair and square, with her own axe!

Furious but unable to break the tradition of his forefathers, Sogon had reluctantly granted Hal's wish to be Iron-Prover and Quartermaster at Atoll Dubh. Hal had heard conversations from the Guards and Sammury of the Atoll's various functions and as his father had been a sword-smith, he knew he could sabotage at least some of the weaponry that was being stockpiled. He'd since survived five assassination attempts and had done a great deal of mischief amongst the stores and had also done his best to provide better food and conditions for the slave-workers at the forges.

"How are you getting along with the Brigand?" asked Gretchen.

"He's no fool and tried to have me killed twice in the first week. By then I'd made three very nice daggers and belt-buckles for him and he warmed to me a bit. All the tested weapons I brought for him to try worked well and what I did was to re-work the same ones to look a little different and continue to put weak layers in the steels of the stockpiled ones. So far no one has realised!"

Gretchen nodded approvingly and said, "If you need to get word to me…" Gretchen then told him of the Ghecko, how to call her, get her to shed some skin for a message and send her on her way.

"Thanks, that's very useful… should've gotten to know you earlier!"

"Better late than never!" she said. "I must get back to my girls. The One continue to guide and protect you."

He was surprised when she embraced and kissed him.

Before turning and striding away, she noticed a Black Guard headed their way. She said in a hushed whisper, "Keep the good weapons close to hand, Hal. You'll need them soon!"

"You bet!" said Hal and calling his foreman-smith, threw a new set of battle-harnesses onto his sleeping shelf. "You know where the spare rations that I stole are kept?"

"Yessir…"

"Break them out after I send this Black Guard on an errand."

"Yessir!"

Gretchen checked that the corridor outside was clear and, running around the corner, nearly collided with Nesbitt who was berating a Black Guard.

Scarcely noticing her, he carried on shouting. "I will not tell you again, Black Guard Nero! Follow the sequence of my orders, not merely their content!" Nesbitt thundered as best as he could but the man had never had either the bearing, nor the voice of an Officer!

Looking where he pointed, Gretchen could see the problem. The Brown Guards had started to repair the damaged outer boarding, before they'd repaired the postwork and structure behind it.

Morons! she thought. If it wasn't for Terrans checking on things, *nothing* would work around here.

Nesbitt now had his back to her and the Black Guard wore an expression of utter contempt and disinterest.

They're really only interested in combat, she thought to herself. 'Blood and Battle' is not only their motto, it's their very reason for existence... poor things.

The chance that Nesbitt could recognise her, even with her change of hair-colour and fake facial scars, was too great a risk, so she quickly back-tracked and left the other caverns and barracks unchecked.

Running as fast and as silently as she could, she was back in her own cavern with the news that everyone was hoping for.

"There's a lot of simple, repairable damage and mess but the main structures are still intact, no corridors breached, no Terran slave-workers in the caverns have been lost and only minor injuries here and there. We've a new friend in the armoury... known well to a good friend of mine. I did hear that two of the lady aristocrats are dead, of the reseal, but one was sent back to Sogon and our Brigand has his new wife... poor soul!"

The girls all laughed.

"Black and Brown guards are dealing with repairs and things... so... with no more ado..."

Pausing and looking at Overseer Brack out of the corner of her eye, he picked up on her cue and shouted, "So... so get back to work, you idle LOOM RATS!"

Putting the best false smile on his face that he could

muster, Brack glanced at Brumuelr by his side and grunted, "Just as I expected, only a little kwak."

"Quake," corrected Brumuelr. "Just as I said, Brumuelr... kwak... yes, just a little... kwak."

"Yes'n of course, Overseer Brack," Brumuelr agreed with little enthusiasm.

Brack continued, "Muster all of our guards. I will hold a full inspection in one hour, of all of you! Reduction in ice-rations and cider if I find any fault in quarters, uniform, weapon, or readiness. Understood?"

Brumuelr jumped back, snapped to attention and looked visibly shaken. "Yes'n, Overseer Brack. I'll see that we's all up'n to Atoll Reg'lation!"

As Brumuelr ran off and cuffed the first two Guards that he came to, Brack shambled back towards to his enclave... fearful... doubtful.

"This doesn't bode well," he muttered to himself. "Had that awful dream again... all my Guards dead... the looms ablaze... the old dead walking..." Despite himself, he looked over the door where Bracks One and Two grinned their death stare down at him. Stooping lower he continued, "Pirates and Navy swarming everywhere they was too... Od's blood, what's amok?"

With all the Blue Guards now running about like headless chickens, preparing for their unexpected full inspection, Gretchen, gathering the girls about her, started to sing very softly.

Soltice ships on our horizon… (Old Sall took up the refrain)
No ice 'n snow 'll stay they moorin' (All now sang)
Davy, Dan and Jacob sing their halyard song,
Pulling loud and pulling long,
Soltice ships, soltice ships be soon arriving,
Time and Tide agree their timing.

In a little world each of their own, through an ethereal mist of time and smoke and for all too brief a moment, all of the loom girls saw their very own soltice ship. All but Old Sall smiled.

"Now girls, haste to your looms," Gretchen said. "Megan and Wendy, give this token to Brown Guard Atilla of the Woodworkers Cavern, and have him send four workers to repair your looms." She handed them a Manifest-token from her skirts and went to her loom to start on what she knew would be her last Tapest… hoped with all her heart would be her last Tapest here.

Hearing a 'click!' she turned and saw Old Sall mouthing to her, Maghoul, I saw, I saw my own soltice ship… it had BLACK sails.

Trust to the One, Maghoul. That it has SAILS is the most important thing! replied Gretchen, with a sweet smile but a heavy heart. She thought on her Benjamin but with matters at hand as they were, she had to quickly dismiss him from her mind but never ever far from her heart.

An ocean away, the Captain flinched and batted away a non-existent fly. "Bother and Barnacles... whatever now..."

"Pardon, Ben?" said Grynne who was standing in his kitchen cupboard-store filling jars, bottles and tins with all manner of stuff. "Was that you or Gretchen just now coming into my mind... blow me down, that was so like her..."

Ben looked at the knife that he had re-hafted and was now sharpening and cleaning. A good one it was too, from Grynne's collection and he was making sure that it was (like all of their gear had to be) in the best possible order. There was more to it than that though, much more than just good kit and tackle. What they were about and what was to be their common fate for the next days (and maybe years) had a focus, a meaning, a *life* to it. It mattered to so many people, whether great and small, whether they knew it yet or not. It was time to address what he had been delaying, what he feared he may do poorly.

"Now my lad..." He put down the whetstone and the knife that he had been sharpening with it. "Sit down over here, my good friend, I've a few things to share with you about the coming battle, the old war, the new one to come, about the One and... our times to be. Pass that Old Ale Flagon over and two good Blackjacks, then sit yourself down nice and comfy, lad. I'll pour."

Grynne frowned. "What do we need two Saps for?"

"Saps? Oh, not fighting Blackjacks, ha ha... yes... you've probably neither heard nor seen such seafarers

'Blackjacks'. Look in that plain wooden sea-chest I just hauled up. It's under your old oil-lamp yonder."

He pointed and Grynne walked over, lifted the lamp and opened the chest. "Oh yes, I see, *tankards*. They're big, aren't they!" He drew two leather tankards that could hold at least two pints each and examined them under the oil-lamp. "Hmm, hard ox-leather, I'd say, lined with tar from the look of it and very... VERY nicely tooled and branded with a fine crest, coat-of-arms and old script."

"My family's crest, Grynne, and one of them is now yours... if you'll accept it?"

Grynne was almost overcome. "Your family... well... yes... thank you, Ben. I don't know quite what to say!" He took the Blackjacks and the flagon over to Ben and sat down next to him as Ben poured from the flagon.

The Captain then talked long into the night and answered all of Grynne's questions, as well as he knew how. Pausing for breath and to whet his dry throat, he saw through the open door, an old and familiar star rising from the east. It was late.

"Well now, Grynne my dear friend, it is time that we were abed and battened down for the night. I have to say you've asked many a fine and searching question and I'm afraid I've not done as much justice to them as I should."

Grynne shook his head and yawned deeply. "Nay Ben, nay, you've answered far more than I asked and things are either now more plain to me, I'd say or... how can I put it? Where other matters are deep and difficult to fathom, I'm content to... to just sail right on over them!"

Ben was taken aback and then laughed loud and long. "Haaaa ha! You've taken a rare and a fine nautical turn-of-phrase to yourself, laddie. That's a good one, 'Sail right on over them'. Ha! You'll make a good seafarer and fine Marine, I've no doubt! There are those who will shortly have every reason to welcome you as shipmate and comrade-in-arms and... those who would tremble if they knew that you were on your way into their devilish and cruel domain!"

Far out to sea at deep water anchor, secure as he could possibly be in his Imperial Battle-Barge Vengeance, concealed and surrounded by the false fogs and mists that his mystic Magi-Schience masters had created at his behest (at the cost of twenty of their own colleagues), Admiree Sogon toyed with his seaweed salad and spiced Whitby shellfish platter. Appetite suddenly and inexplicably gone, he snapped his fingers. The dishes were instantly removed and new wine and dainties put in their place. He glared at the brim-full obsidian goblet and dishes. Too distracted now to rebuke his servitors, he rose and strode to the windows of his stateroom.

"The divination cup." His understated and barely audible order nevertheless had servitors all but falling over themselves to bring the cup, covered with its richly embroidered veil from the Temple-Altar, to where he now stood at the Gun-head windows. Nodding to the small shelf by the leaded window, where the cup was speedily placed, he put out his left hand and scooped up the ancient tokens of his ancestral people from a highly polished and jewel-encrusted Terran skull. Straightening his back and hiding the very real fear of what he was about to do, he closed both eyes, raised his right hand to the mystic and merciful heavens of his Emperor-Gods and with lowered head whispered in his mother-tongue, "Aaswe, kuu noa an hass. Aaswe pushwe an hass. Riiven!"

He placed the tokens in the cup and turned to the Woejin Board. Swirling the cup, he closed his eyes and tipped the tokens onto the board. Some fell on the floor and were therefore not worthy of consideration. With a sharp intake of breath, he opened his eyes and as Admiree, Plenipotentiary and Defender of the Peoples of the East, he looked to the wishes and doom of his Emperor-Gods.

Three ships lay right-side up with another two more upside-down. Both of them were just touching a red fire-leaf and one also touched a small polished stone. Inside the 'curtilage' section of the board, two empty walnut-shells lay right side up and one upside down. Two more lay outside, up-ended, and between them was a Tree of Life! For him to attack with the main fleet was certain (as previously foretold) but what about his reserve forces? Other tokens spread over the board, repeated some earlier advice and obscure warnings but "Gods and Demons!" once again there was the one heart-shaped Breadfruit, right in the centre of the board and all but covering his personal crest-piece. A new grey-green feather (strangely reminiscent) also lay on the board, swirling lazily in a draught. He'd seen this before but where? Biting down on an oath and withholding a rebuke to his servants, he gazed long and hard at the feather which suddenly just blew into the fire and burned up.

"Wine!" Another strident whisper brought the cup instantly to his hand. Draining it in one, he turned to the Black Guard at the doorway. "Summon my Commanders to the chart-room and bring my wives to me. The rest of you, leave." As the doors closed, he could not but shiver as he gazed through the leaded windows of his unsinkable Battle-Barge and coldly surveyed the false mists that surrounded them... whilst none could see in, neither could he see out.

8. Blades and Trades

"I'd better take a short carbine as well as the long-rifle. Hmmm, maybe the double barrel shotgun too. I don't think one trunk is going to be enough now." Grynne was mumbling to himself, as he bent over the sea-chest, around which was scattered all manner of weapons, kit and caboodle. He shouted over his shoulder, "Captain! Is it alright to take the guns in a sailcloth kit-bag, if I wrap them in blanket, or should they go in the chest?"

The Captain ambled over, munching on a purple carrot, and took the kit bag and inspected it carefully. He pulled hard on the shoulder strap and peered inside, holding it up to the light to check for holes or loose stitching; he seemed satisfied. "Put wooden rods cut to length down the barrels to protect them, wrap each in a towel and take plenty of oil and cleaning cloths. When we're under way, I'll show you how to make a battle-valise for them, with that oiled-canvas you have. Don't forget your best sewing kit and thread. Nice carrots!"

The Captain returned to the larder, where he continued to pack food, spices and herbs. He checked each tin or jar in turn, emptying two into one, mixing a few here and there and replacing the rest, that were not suited to sea-voyages, on the shelves.

"I'm taking at least one month's supplies with us. We can re-stock at Admiralty Atoll, and we'll fish as we sail. You always get birds landing in the ship, we'll pot the tastiest as we like," he called out to Grynne who was wrapping his long-rifle. He took a bottle of wine with no label from a shelf, popped the cork and sniffed. "Mmm… that'll do." So saying, he poured two good measures into earthenware chalices for himself and for Grynne.

"How many musket balls and shot should I take?"

"How many have you got!"

Grynne pointed to the left of the door. "They're all on the floor in that green box, Ben."

The Captain knelt down and pulled out a beautifully inlaid mahog-wood box with gold hinges and clasps.

Some exceptional things have washed-up on your shore, Grynne my lad, thought the Captain to himself. I've only once seen such a box, in the Ambassador's hall, when he accepted a gift from the last Orient trader, to visit before the massacre. That was sent by Sogon, that was. He thought bitterly and fingered the curling snake in gold, jade and sea lion ivory on the lid, recognising Sogon's crest! Was it the same as the one on the old faded sword-scabbard on the wall, that he'd seen on his first morning in the cabin with Grynne?

He gaped open-mouthed at the crest of the most famous and cruel Orient General of the last five hundred years and leapt to his feet. Running back into the room, he tripped over a pile of foul-weather oilskins and, barely regaining his balance, skidded into the wall by the window.

Grynne turned to face him.

"Blow me down… is that…? That crest, that crest!" Ben pointed to the sword in front of him. Torn though the covering of the scabbard was, there indeed was a faded crest, the curling snake of Sogon's ancestral family. "A snake curling around a ball, a globe, some say the world itself. Sogons' crest!" He ran his fingers over the design.

Grynne was astonished. "Sogon's crest, you mean to say it was his?"

Ben continued to stare at the sword and its scabbard and as he stroked his beard and rubbed at his eye-patch, the seconds grew to minutes. "What? His! Oh no… no… more like… more than likely it was his father's or one of his uncles'. The rest of the embroidery is gone… gone…" He stroked over the tooled-leather and silver-work. "Title and first name are not here…" He let his arm drop and shook his head. "Sorry, lad, it was such… such a shock to see it after all these years, first on that box in there and to realise that you had one of his family's swords. You of all people. HA! You, it had to be you, Grynne me boy. You'll be taking that with you and I'll give you special lessons!"

"Captain, ermm, Ben, you said earlier and I meant to ask, but there's been so much to do and so much is spinning around in my head. You said that, that old Oragoratory bird out there, would have taken word to Sogon… to Sogon at Atoll Dubh? Am I right in saying that… Sogon's got Gretchen at Atoll Dubh?"

The Captain waved his hand, shook his head and responded, "Yes, he has her after a fashion but he's not at Atoll Dubh, I'll wager, and even if he has met her, he wouldn't know who she is. He's in his Battle-Barge somewhere… somewhere safe and distant if I know his style. Gretchen is at Attol Dubh though, my lad. Does that... disturb you?"

Grynne's face was set like flint. "Disturb?" His fists were clenched so tight the veins stood out. "Disturb is not the word, Captain..." A wry smile split his handsome features. "I just wonder if you'd be displeased... if I got my hands on him before you did."

It took but a split-second for the Captain to roar with laughter. "HA HA! Good lad, good master Grynne. If you get to him first... if you get there first, he'll be surrounded by his personal Sammury, all of them as fast and as deadly as green vipers. If you get there first..." He looked to the floor and then to the ceiling as if searching for an old memory. "If you get there first, take your time. Slow down as you approach, there'll be traps, tricks and even Magi-Schience against you. If it were me (and by the One, I hope it is me), I'd take his men, one at a time and not look him in the eye. He can't attack a man who doesn't lay an eye on him. That is his code of honour, black-hearted devil that he is... he will not break the code of his forefathers." He lifted the sword and its scabbard from the wall and slid the old blade out and gave a dazzling display of sword-play, sword in his right hand and scabbard in his left. Then in an instant, sword and scabbard were swopped from hand-to-hand and he performed another astonishing series of moves. He paused and looked first at Grynne and then back to the weapons still hung on the walls. "Do you have either use for, or liking, for that broadsword?" He nodded towards an old Pictish broadsword, hanging by a thong at the doorpost.

"No… no, why, do you want it?" answered Grynne.

In answer, the Captain slashed three times at the broadsword and sparks flew into every corner of the room. There were three 'clangs' as severed blade pieces hit the floor. Drawing back slightly, he dropped the scabbard, held the hilt of Sogon's sword in both hands and using his full body-weight and strength, stabbed at what was left of the broadsword, just below its hilt. Another spray of sparks flew from the doorpost.

Grynne had shielded his eyes from the sparks with his hands. As the air grew thick with the smell of scorched iron and carbon and as the blue haze began to clear, he saw to his astonishment three fragments of the broadsword blade on the floor, each cut clean. Clean as a slice of purple carrot.

The Captain backed away from the doorway, rubbing and waving both of his hands. "Ouch… that hurt," he said.

The Sammury sword seemed to shimmer and flex like a reed. It was plunged deep into the door post, *through* the broadsword's blade, just below its hilt, where the metal was thickest.

"My… my… word." Grynne stood gazing until the haze of carbon smoke caught the back of his throat. He coughed, retched and accepted the chalice of wine that the Captain offered him, taking a deep swig.

"That blade goes with you as your main personal side-arm, and no discussion," said Ben, as they both stood gazing at the astonishing sight. "Remarkable Damasced-steel it is. They say that the blacksmiths used Magi-Schience in the making of it. Aye, that blade goes with you, Grynne my lad… of course first of all, you'll have to get it out of the doorpost!"

The Captain drained half of his chalice of wine and returned to his task of packing rations (or vittles as he called them) for the journey.

Grynne spent a good five minutes trying unsuccessfully to recover the sword from the doorpost. Sweat ran down his nose and he heard a giggle from the larder. Irritated, he recalled something that the Captain had said earlier down on the beach during their sword-fighting practice. 'Where strength fails and can only fail… resort to reason!' Now let's see. This is just impossible. Even if that blade is as sharp as sharp can be. No man has the strength to push metal through metal. The Captain's strong, but I'm stronger, much stronger and I just can't get that blade out of the post or out of the blade of that broadsword. The blade *must have a strength of its own.* Maybe I'm holding it awry. He put his hands on the hilt and tried to hold it in a different way. This time he held gently, rather than gripping the hilt forcefully or in anger. The blade shifted slightly and there was a slight grinding sound as it came slightly out of the broadsword. He stopped, amazed at his own insight. He held the hilt again and gently… slowly drew the blade clear of doorpost and broadsword. The blade in his hand shimmered and rang like a small bell. It was unmarked! Point and blade had not a scratch, nor a dent, nor a blemish. He put the point of the blade back against the broadsword and pushed hard. It went in a little way, sparks falling onto the floor. Pushing harder still, it went right through and he could feel heat coming from the metal. Pulling hard, the sword stayed where it was. Pulling gently, he retrieved it easily. The hilt of the old broadsword, now released, swung upside down and fell onto the floor with a crash.

The Captain's voice came from the larder. "Very well-reasoned, Grynne... very well-reasoned. Put that sword back in its scabbard now and stow it in your kit bag."

"Yes, yes, I will, but Ben, this is the weapon of an expert. Don't you want it?"

"Bless you, lad, that's a kind thought, but there's no need. I already have one of the seven." He then strode into the room holding the green box with Sogon's crest. He set the heavy box on a cluttered table and, freeing the clasps, opened the lid with some care. Taking out a small box of shot and some musket balls in a linen bag, he paused and looked over at Grynne who was examining and stroking the blade very carefully.

Ben thought to himself, now is the time, and drawing a deep breath he spoke.

"There were seven great Masterii Smithmen, fine craftsmen they were. Many years past, they were brought from every corner of the globe. Some as a result of warfare, others by subterfuge or kidnap or by choice, thinking on what riches and status they might gain. They all then laboured for the great dynasty of the Orient Emperors and produced the finest of weapons for their aristocracy. Not just swords, you understand, but bows and many other such things. That was before guns were thought of, of course." He took a last swig from his bottle and set it carefully on a shelf. Wiping his beard with the back of his hand, he continued, "The story, more than legend tells that one feast day when most of them were drunken, all but one of the Masterii fell into a dispute with the others. Each slandered the others' skill and said that they knew nothing of fine metalwork or of the ancient crafts of their own fathers. In their own native tongues and dialects, they declared their secrets to the group, believing that the others could not understand. The one Masterii (Baliol by name) realised that he only knew their tongues and dialects and he quietly fed the dispute with more wines and a malice all of his own. By the end of that day, he knew all of their secrets and committed them to his own craft-parchments. Time passed and he committed it all to memory and he then burned those parchments. Unwisely, he told the Emperor of this. The Emperor (that was Sogon's grandfather), then commanded the Masterii-Smiths to work together, using all of their combined skills to produce one perfect sword each. Each had two apprentices and those apprentices were all commanded to make the scabbards, plus two matching knives. They were to make them by the next Summer Solstice evening. At the same time by his command, a new mausoleum was commissioned to be built in the palace grounds, next to the blacksmiths quarter. It seems that they did not understand the… errmm… *significance* of this. On the day of the Solstice, their preparations were almost complete and as the Emperor's family gathered to feast, they set to their final process. You have to understand, Grynne, that the final tempering of a blade is the most crucial. You know of this?"

"Yes," said Grynne. "The blade must be heated several times to an exact heat and then plunged into something cool like water or oil to give it its final strength. I read of this in an old book."

Ben looked grim. "It has always been the way of the Orient's Masterii to do the final temper… in a body. Usually that of an animal or a criminal."

"Oh my word!" said Grynne.

Ben nodded. "I think you're ahead of me, lad. Those Masterii didn't know it until too late but they were to provide their own final tempering. The 'icing on the cake' was, so to speak, that they were all buried with their apprentices in a mausoleum of a kind usually reserved for the Emperors themselves. I hope they appreciated the… errmm… kind thought!" He gave a wry smile. "So then, their individual and collective secrets died with them and their apprentices and those twenty-one swords and daggers remained in the hands of the families of the Emperors until one by one, they were lost at sea, taken in battle or by intrigue and treachery. Even weapons like that are of little use against an arrow in the back, nor Hellbane-liqour in your wine! Sogon's family eventually lost their titles as Emperors through unwise plans and failed warfare and he is now the only surviving male descendant to retain any title. He styles himself as 'Admiree' which offends not their aristocracy too much. If he succeeds in what we believe is his plan though, he'll take the Emperor's position, style himself 'Battle Lord' or most likely 'Defender of the Peoples of the East' and try to take possession of the entire globe, leaving no enemies behind. To achieve this with no visible army at home, he would need to 'Make' a huge warrior clan using the ancient and dark Magi-Schiences of the past. One of the tale-legends, which I noted during my research at the Admiralty, used antique and more 'workaday or farming-talk' than usual. There were a whole bunch of words which had the meanings almost like 'warriors' or 'soldiers' but they had constructs, accents and suffixes more commonly used for mythical beasts of the field, water-buffalo with men's faces, labourers and the like. You do understand the difference between past, present and future accents in the Greek, lad?"

Grynne nodded.

"Well, those passages held an antique past tense plus future accents. That was what led me to understand that the legend of the Beast-Men created by Magi-Schience was most likely true. The rest of that tale held that they do not have a man's capacity for thought and reason but are very strong and loyal to their clan-chiefs, very much like a herd of cattle. As I understand from what Gretchen sent us, they take real animal flesh and bone and re-mold them into man-like beasts. They have a small whaling-fleet based at the Atoll and I've no doubt but that whales, orcas and the like, are their 'base' materials…"

Grynne shuddered as Ben continued.

"Grynne, my lad, we'll be facing beast-men. 'Guards' they are called, bigger than most men and women soldiers that any have seen, stronger and trained for battle, but they seem to lack memory as much as they lack a true family. What they don't learn and re-learn every sweep of a full moon, they often forget… including how to fight."

Grynne remained silent for a long time, gazing at his feet and then said, "Can we use that against them? Delay their training somehow, let them get… sloppy?"

Ben beamed and nodded as Grynne continued.

"If we get there early on a low tide, I slip in to meet Gretchen, somehow disrupt their re-training and then we all make landfall later and then take them on."

Ben looked puzzled. "How would you achieve such a stratagem?"

"In my Qajaq, my sea-going canoe. It floated ashore years ago, rather damaged but I repaired it and I've learned how to use it well for fishing in all weathers. The fortress is on an atoll, a small islet, you say? I can easily paddle in under darkness and land, do what I can and then return. If there's ice and fire in the seas, there'll be a lot of mist. I've often been out all night fishing in that kayak…" He pointed now to the sealskin Qajaq hung under a lean-to at the end of the garden. "In all kinds of weather… sometimes by choice!" His last witticism went unnoticed by Ben.

Now Ben fell silent and gazed at his feet. He mouthed calculations under his breath. "Moon on this last quarter... two standard weeks... four days to... at least forty Marines... twenty-four men on the rigging... two hours at least... seven at most... I wonder if we could find Medulla's squad of Doomed-men?" He muttered some more, counted on his fingers, then said, "Yes, my boy! Good master Grynne, we now have a plan!"

"We do?"

"Yes, laddie, we do!"

Some two weeks' sail away, Fleet-Captain Jamsetjee Gryffen-Wadia (Jammy, to his senior staff and friends) studied the bay and his small fleet that lay before him and tapped lightly on his chilled bottle of Chardonnay. Nice and cool it was now, after a quarter of an hour in his old battered ice-bucket. He poured himself a glass and took a long, deep draught.

"Mmm very good!"

A half-eaten small fish, a Skate or Ray, coated in beer-batter and fried in beef dripping, lay in a bowl at his side. The salad was good, not as good as from his kitchen-garden back in Old Blighty... but good. The midday cannon was due to fire sometime soon.

In the bay of his Atoll, two frigates, three cutters and several skiffs and a barge lay at anchor or lashed to the quay. Long-boats and a dozen or more small jolly-boats lay on skids or upside-down on the repair-racks. One frigate was always-half-manned and ready to slip anchor at a moment's notice. Two newcomers, The Weaver, a deep-water trader-barque armed with a dozen cannon plus its sister-ship also a trader, The Tailor, also lay at anchor in the middle of the bay. All in all, it was as impressive a sight as it was picturesque. Jammy never tired of it. The trader had a skiff at the quayside with boxes of goods and there was brisk trade going on with the marines, tradesmen, seamen, a few pirates plus their wives and children.

He topped up his glass and then pushed the bottle deeper into the ice and took up his Northumran Pipes. Putting the bellows under his left forearm, he pumped twice and when it felt just right, he started to play, 'The races at the Whitby towns, June the 17th 1777', a tune of his own devising. More or less in the key of A minor and not quite in rhythm.

In the ante-room next door and painfully within earshot, his PLO (Pirate Liaison Officer) Ensign Gregor clamped hands over his ears. "I was mare fond of that-there cat when it yowled afore it died and became that... that... thing!"

Pirate First Mate Bristol, the ALO (Admiralty Liaison Officer), laughed at his side. "I do allow that there malady is'n a few notes short of a toon, an' as amir resemblance to a strangled-beast's last cry in the air this day!"

The two men laughed and each took a swig out of a small flagon of contraband rum.

Nearby sailors and marines normally indolent at

midday, hearing the cacophony leapt to their feet and ran to the exercise yards and nets. Games of pitch and toss, three-legged-Percy, wrestling and sword-play broke out in the barracks and beyond. Laughter (but mostly curses) echoed around the armoury walls as the 'tune' lifted its anti-melodious cacophony to the heavens above. Then suddenly, mid-tune, it stopped!

So did everything else! A long minute passed. Men looked at each other but said nothing… then, a melodious, a very melodious, bird-song…

Gregor looked hesitantly around the door.

"Did you hear that!?" shouted his Fleet-Captain.

Gregor jumped! "Why, yes… yes… it's one of… my… favourites…"

"Belay that lie and fall in a cutter-crew of eight seamen and marines, senior Coxswain Jellico to lead. A full week's rations with a standard barrel of small beer, full rigging, foul-weather gear and standard weapons. Jump to it NOW, man!"

"Aye aye, Fleet!"

"And a swivel-gun at the prow!" he added as Gregor ran for the barracks.

Not a man to delay any task, the Fleet-Captain hurriedly put pen and ink to the Ghecko-skin in his hand and folding it quickly, tied it to the Blue-Ocean Hawk's leg. The Hawk had almost finished eating what was left of his skate, he then noted with amusement. He blew it a kiss from a safe distance and the Hawk wiped beak on claw, blinked at him in thanks, shook itself, flapped once to

137

the open window, caught the afternoon on-shore breeze and… disappeared.

Gretchen's note to him had been brief. *'Jammy, find Ninja-Queen Julianna and call all that are hers to you. My Benjy en-route, Medulla aware. Havoc! Gretchy X'*

So, what she had told him of Sogon's intentions when she had passed through two years or more ago, was most likely true!

Slightly more excited now than 'a-feared', Jammy looked southwards and spoke aloud.

"Thought it couldn't be too long now. It's been two years or so since she set sail for…"

His PLO Gregor stood panting at the door.

"And? Ah yes, you'll, actually no, they'll need a heading and orders." A slight pause for thought. "Send Coxswain Jellico to me now. There'll be no written orders, it's off the books, fetch me the ready-cash box."

Over across the bay just now, Coxswain Caleb Jellico reclined at his ease at the old mussel-stall, under the shadow of the Pirates Halls, the old Naval and Army Prison still known affectionately as the 'Scrubs'. Susie Tegan-Pierce-Rees, the wife of the Pirate Captain, and he were in deep conversation as her children played 'Short-stop Jinny' at their feet, with dice and skittles.

Caleb was speaking. "…she had the most beautiful eyes, lovely long hair and I could tell that she was… interested in me but the whole thing was just full of… danger and then I noticed that she was armed to the teeth! It was such a strange dream."

"Sounds jus' loik I used t' be, afore I met yon layabout Captin 'Silly'!" Susie laughed and added, "…don't thee as dare tell 'im I told yus that's wit I call him private-like… Sylvester be his given-name t' be sure but e's alus 'Silly' tae me!"

They both laughed again.

"If'n it's strange dreams ye're 'avin Oi'd lay off'n the razor-shell-fish and winkles if'n I wus thee!" She nodded to the paper bag in which Caleb's purchases lay.

Before Caleb could reply, his attention was distracted not by the anticipated midday cannon but by three long whistle blasts from the quayside.

"That's 'Coxswain to the Captain' signal. I'd best be off now, Susie. Bye kids, play nicely now." He patted the smaller ones on the head as he left and a few steps away he spun on his heels and said, "Bethan, take the two red skittles with that three on the dice, you'll get double-points on the rack!"

As he ran to his jolly-boat, he heard the skittles crash and shouts from the children went up.

"Dat be a ringer fur sure!"

"T'irty points tae us'n an' ye're laggin' lanky-breeches… Ha!"

"Dat's not FAIR yu's cheated wi' dat Cox'n!"

"It IS in d' rules… moi rules!"

A fight broke out.

Fights always broke out when 'Short-stop Jinny' was

played but Susie didn't mind the odd bruise or a bloody nose. Her children had to learn the ways of the world, the lore of the sea and mostly, learn how to fight! Most often the girls won anyway, which pleased her immensely.

Not an hour later, somewhat a-feared, Coxswain Jellico plus eight somewhat puzzled sailors and Marines set sail north-eastwards. They were headed to the far bay of that great river, the Hesperance from which he had once fled for his life, along with Lieutenant Benjamin Golightly-Witherspoon and the other survivors of the fall of the Fortress of Louis the Unlucky. Bad memories and anger all but kept him from careful navigation through the shoals and rocks of the eastern defences.

He had been given gold-coin to barter for food or help, should he need it. He could be back soon or not! He had been told that there was no telling if she (Ninja-Queen Julianna, her Ninja-girls and family) would still be where they were a year ago, or even alive when they got there and no telling if they'd be welcome either! How old would Julianna be now?

Fleet-Captain Gryffen-Wadia made a list of orders to give verbatim to his men that night at Muster and then wrote a mostly fictitious report to the Admiralty, mentioning an outbreak of the Ague and Gum-fever, a small but significant fire to the armoury and yet another loss to the fleet of a cutter, during an engagement with a marauding privateer, which they had nevertheless sunk. He added,

'Can we have a real dentist on secondment next time'. A long list of required provisions, powder and shot, sail-canvas, tools and timber was appended. Knowing that he'd be lucky to get a quarter of what he asked, he signed the parchment and added a hot-wax seal with his signet ring. He appended short missives and notes to be sent on to his family, plus a private letter to Admiral-Quartermaster Tim Jones-Parry, asking him to visit his cousin Henry, licensee at the Black Bear in Camden Town. This letter gave his permission for his sister Havoc, to marry.

He had no sister Havoc of course but his cousin Henry receiving this news with the word 'Havoc', would take all close and aged family to safety to the far Northern Islands and Henry would notify the 'Fellowship of the Fortresses' (a secret society of serving and retired Admiralty and Army personnel), that war on a global scale was most likely.

"Ensign Gregor!"

"Yes, Fleet?"

"Take a skiff and two men, have them row you over to Mr Harris on the Weaver and ask him if he would be so kind as to join me immediately, for afternoon tea. Also, before you go, tell cook that I'll be entertaining Mr Harris and that he is to lay out the finest spread as he can muster."

Less than an hour later, the Fleet-Captain and his old friend Merchant-Mariner Captain Harris had enjoyed the very finest that the Admiralty could offer south of the equator. William Harris stretched back in his chair and asked, "So Jammy, my old lad, that was indeed a fine and delicious repast and so tell me now, what will it cost me?"

"I need you to set sail with your own and your sister's merchant ship, back to Old Blighty on tomorrow's high tide."

"That's a tall order, Jammy. We're not due to slip our moorings till next Wednesday. We await an Orient trader with silks and fine furniture anytime soon."

Jammy sat forward and looked deep into his friend's eyes. "We go back a long way, don't we, Bill? You were one of the last merchant vessels to leave before the Fortress on the Hesperance fell... and... if it's Orient goods you await, you may get more than you bargained for but... you may have the same luck again... if you leave tomorrow."

The old man bent quickly forward. "The Fortress... Orients... tomorrow... what on Terra is afoot, Jammy?"

"I can say no more, my dear friend, other than this..." He put a leather and oil-cloth valise into the old man's hand. "Make sure... *absolutely sure* that these reach the Admiralty and my cousin as soon as possible."

Harris looked at the valise in his hand and slowly nodded. "That I will... ermm... Jammy, I'll leave gold for my goods, if the Orient trader should..."

Jammy raised his hand and interrupted, "If your goods arrive in your absence, I'll have them put into safe storage. If I and my men survive, we'll have another fine meal when you next return to collect them."

"If!" spluttered William.

The two men stood and William held out two shaky hands and grasped his friend by the shoulders. "We'll beat every record back to Old Blighty and... and... be careful and successful, old friend, in whatever it is you have to do!" He nodded and they embraced.

"Ensign Gregor! Our guest is taking his leave of us. We will both walk with him to your skiff and then convey him to his boat. When you return, appraise our Admiralty Liaison Officer First Mate Bristol to convey my compliments to Pirate Captain Sylvester Tegan-Rees and bid him to join me this evening for supper in my chambers."

The short walk down to the quayside was uncharacteristically silent, thought Ensign Gregor. The two old friends waved to each other as the skiff pulled away and each one wondered whether in this life, they would meet again.

What their Fleet-Captain told his squadron and Marines later that evening (after double rations, old ale and tarred tobacco) had them standing and cheering! The next day however when sober, many were strangely quieted as they bent to their tasks.

Pirate Captain Sylvester Tegan-Pierce-Rees had left the Fleet Captain's supper earlier that evening with a spring in his step. He thought, One more time, me'be t' last time... (which was okay, he had no desire to die a-bed) ...tae lead ma crew intae battle far-further south than us've ever bin afore intae t' frozen-ocean where fire an' danger an' glory lie!

He knew he would have to make but little effort to spur his men and maids to jump to their preparations!

9. Hopes and Heart-Songs

Gretchen sat in her small stall in the upper galleries that housed the other Loom-girls, artisans, metal-workers, trades peoples and labourers in the slave-quarter. Megan was cooking the meal for their 'Six', just outside. All her girls were organised in Sixes. She had re-organised all of the trades in groups of six on the Atoll, only she and a few others knew why and they never spoke openly of it.

Old Sall sighed and said, "I do hope it's not venison tonight!"

"No… and not Scots beef neither!" piped-up Shelagh-no-tears.

Free to talk properly now, the chatter of the womenfolk was loud over the general din of hundreds of slaves around them. As Megan stirred the bubbling stew and prodded the few small potatoes in the other dixie, others joined in, saying that they hoped it wouldn't be salmon, lamb, bacon, or exotic vegetables.

Nearby 'Sixes' caught up again on the old joke and some shouted over, "No, you don't want to be eating any of that rotten stuff!"

"Stap that for vittles, girls. I'd hate it to be prawns and spicy-rice tonight!"

"So what is it then, Megan?" Gretchen said. "What culinary delight have you got for us tonight?"

Megan smiled. "Had to walk all the way to Bangalore for this!"

"Ooo, you'll have got your feet wet on that trip!" laughed old Sall.

"Tort you wus gon a fare toime," added Aiko.

"Yes, me dears, you can't jist go out an' get whale meat any time you jist take a mind to!"

"Ooo, whale-meat. My favourite!"

"Wat a treet, the meat of the big fellow his-self."

"Can't remember the last time I ate whale meat. I do hope it was rotten and stringy when you got it."

"Of course, me dears, don't I always get the worst of the catch, just to treat you all like princesses of the realm."

They laughed together.

Everyone in that cavern would eat whale meat stew with seaweeds and a few small potatoes, that night. It was the same every day. The only difference in the Sixes was that Gretchen's girls could laugh and make a joke of it. Gretchen's girls went to sleep at night with a song in their heart. Another outbreak of the 'Auld Scurvy' had been the talk of the armoury and metalworkers' talk that night and they were in an ill humour, in every sense of the word.

"I've a special treat for you all tonight, girls…" Gretchen's voice took on a more melodious lilt. "…one which I think you'll appreciate."

Karis made to respond but realised that Gretchen was serious.

Sunita (always slow to catch onto the general drift of a conversation) didn't pick up on the inflexion in Gretchen's tone and said, "I see she's found an old dog-bone to stir the mess with, Ha!"

Gretchen smiled sweetly. "Has no one noticed what I'm sitting upon?" She drew her skirts to one side.

"That's surely not full, no, it couldn't…"

"It can't be!"

"Look you now, 'tis leekin'a touch…"

"Merciful heavens!"

"How the deuce… you little divil…"

Gretchen gave the barrel upon which she sat, a sharp Rap! with her knuckles. The dull and deep noise therefrom, confirmed that she was indeed sat upon a full barrel, a *very* full barrel of cider.

Karis said, "Old Sall can have my share, I don't drink alkyhol."

Old Sall smiled broadly.

"Hush and shush, my dears, this is for us Loom-girls only. A pint, or a little more each after we've danced! I dearly wish we could give every one of us slave-workers a drink but the coming fray is upon us mostly (that is we'll be starting the fight), inside the Fortress and this is to help stave off the Scurvy. We must be in fine fettle from now on until help arrives…"

The girls stared at her with a mixture of elation, fear, astonishment and sheer hunger.

"We'll 'delay' our meal tonight… spread the word quietly, let the other slave-workers in their own caverns cook and clear their places and then we'll share my 'spoils' of the day equally with all of us Loom-girls. I'll tell you later how I obtained this ermm, medicine."

Quietly and quickly the girls scattered with the news

whilst Gretchen stirred the stew and set it aside. She then led the Loom-girls in the dance and then stood to one side, watching intently. One by one she called the girls and gave each a new instruction, a variation on a step, a higher jump required, a kick or a punch extra in the routine. After another few minutes she called "STOP!"

"Old Sall… attack me kicking, anyway you chose.

Aisha… come at me from behind, try to choke me.

Shelagh… try to throw me off-balance…"

Gretchen's commands rolled off her tongue as smoothly and smartly as the girls' own responses were! They attacked, withdrew, picked-up-apace and repeated. As she parried their blows and kicks, she pushed them into the four quadrants of the room…

"You three, free-wheel…

You two wrestle and throw…

Anya, Helena and Jackie throw punches…"

After a long time, she called, "Cease, cease, CEASE!"

The girls stood panting, rubbing their bruised arms, legs and the odd bleeding lip!

"That… that was truly the BEST display that I have ever seen! Come sit ye down… you've earned your reward, twice, thrice, many times over! Sunita, put the pot back on to the fire to warm-up."

Rubbing her own bruised arms and hands, she went over to the barrel and hoisted it onto a bench. Shelagh-no-tears didn't have to be told to bring cups and mugs from the cleaning troughs in an old Trogg-basket.

"Hand those around, girls, and stand in line. Once I open this, it'll just keep pouring."

Checking that they were all ready, she flexed her back, clenched her left fist and almost too fast to see, gave the bung in the top of the barrel such a blow that sent it into the barrel itself! BANG! A spurt of cider splashed across her face. Without a flinch, she shifted her stance, put her right hand onto her hip and extended her middle-finger. She squinted, glared at the side of the barrel where ordinarily a Tap and Spile would be hammered in at the Spile-bung, for drawing cider in a tavern. They had no such thing. Taking a deep breath and hunching-forward (it seemed that she hadn't moved at all... if not for the jet of cider coming from the barrel and her, "...OUCH! That hurt more than I thought!"), there would have been no evidence that she had in point-of-fact punched the spile-bung into the barrel with a single finger.

Shelagh-no-tears put her own mug under the stream of sparkling amber liquid and then stood aside as the other girls filled their own assorted and various drinking-vessels in turn. She watched as Gretchen licked her finger and then pronounced, "Quite good quality, I'd say."

How does she do things like that? was the thought on every Loom-girls' mind.

Sunita also gave her allotment to another of the Loom-girls, Blainad, who grinned and drained it in one. "Jist loike moi dada tort-me... Hic!"

There was just enough left in the barrel for Gretchen to fill her own mug, once and only once every other girl had taken a share. None but a mildly embarrassed Blainad had taken a sip.

"Bless you one and all, my sisters. May the One and the kind gods you love, bless your hearts!"

Sailte Gretchen

Kippis!

Cheer to yus ALL

Salut

Bottoms-upsy!

Bon apitit…

In the heart-language of their mothers, they toasted one another and following the traditions of their peoples, they sniffed, sipped, drained, swilled, supped and swallowed the sweet, fiery cider. Grins grew bigger, eyes wider, hiccups longer and knees became a 'tad' more wobbly!

The evening meal was then served to all in wooden bowls, worn smooth by spoons and fingers. It did not take long till all of the stew was gone and the girls sat or sprawled on the floor.

"Bhhuuurrpp," came from Old Sall.

"Couldn't have put it better meself," opinioned Shelagh-no-tears, patting her own chest, with a deep rumble from a bit lower down. "Yes, quite a good quality I'd say… and girls…"

They all looked to her.

"Here's to the finest of the produce of your homelands, that you'll all drink again of one fine day… and that right soon!"

So saying, Gretchen drained her mug and all the others

Masterii: Craftsmen of mystic arts. Magicians.

Sammury: Warrior class of the Orient Peoples.

Legerdemain: Sleight of hand, deception.

Maghoul: Term of warm affection between good friends.

Ghecko: A small amphibian/reptile with special abilities.

Creels: Woven baskets of various sizes and purposes.

Judoka: Martial-arts trained warrior.

Ninja: Martial-arts trained warrior.

Dixies: Large cooking-pots.

Birk: A common term for any kind of boat or ship.

Brae: Hillside or other open area.